S0-DLD-440

WEEKLY READER BOOKS presents

A UFO Has Landed

Milton Dank & Gloria Dank

dp

Delacorte Press/New York

Published by
Delacorte Press
1 Dag Hammarskjold Plaza
New York, N.Y. 10017

Copyright © 1983 by Milton Dank and Gloria Dank

All rights reserved.
No part of this book may be reproduced or
transmitted in any form or by any means, electronic or
mechanical, including photocopying, recording, or by any
information storage and retrieval system, without the written
permission of the Publisher, except where permitted by law.

Manufactured in the United States of America

First printing

Designed by Richard Oriolo

LIBRARY OF CONGRESS CATALOGING IN PUBLICATION DATA

Dank, Milton [date of birth]
A UFO has landed.
Summary: When their biology teacher is in danger of being
dismissed because he insists that he saw a UFO and some aliens,
the Galaxy Gang sets out to help Mr. Dawson by gathering
evidence to prove his strange story.
[1. Unidentified flying objects—Fiction.   2. School stories.
3. Mystery and detective stories]   I. Dank, Gloria. II. Title.
III. Title: UFO has landed.
PZ7.D228Uf   1983   [Fic]   82-18353
ISBN 0-385-29297-X

This book is a presentation of
Weekly Reader Books.
Weekly Reader Books offers book clubs for children
from preschool through junior high school.
For further information write to:
Weekly Reader Books
4343 Equity Drive
Columbus, Ohio 43228

Edited for Weekly Reader Books and published
by arrangement with Delacorte Press

For Randy

1

☐ "Did he really see a UFO?" Chessie asked. Her eyes sparkled, and she bounced excitedly on her grandstand seat. The rumor about the new biology teacher had swept through the school this Monday morning, creating a sensation. Now, at lunch time, the Galaxy Gang was meeting at the playing field to talk about it.

Diggy zipped up his windbreaker against the chilly October breeze and shook his head. "It's just a rumor," he said, "the sort of thing the newspapers are making a big fuss over lately. You know—mysterious blips on radar, fast-moving lights, someone who says he was kidnapped and taken to Venus."

"The surface temperature on Venus," Sphinx said, "is something like eight hundred degrees Fahrenheit. I bet that kept him on his toes."

Diggy ignored the interruption. "Anyway, Mr. Dawson's a real scientist. He wouldn't believe in that sort of stuff."

There was a pause while the gang thought this over. For the past two weeks there had been a rash of UFO sightings in the Philadelphia area. People were nervous and some almost hysterical at the possibility of alien visitors. One man had even rushed into a city council meeting screaming that he was being bombarded by deadly rays from outer space. And if the rumor was true, Mr. Dawson had certainly seen *something*.

Bobbie pulled her blond pigtails up like antennae. "Little bubble-headed men saying 'Take me to your leader.' Forget it! Diggy's right. Mr. Dawson wouldn't believe in that stuff. It's just another crazy rumor—like that one about Old Hairy getting the Nobel Prize."

The gang laughed as they remembered the shock of Mrs. Harriet Swindell, English 2A, when people started congratulating her on winning the big prize. Someone had printed up a phony newspaper headline announcing the award and posted it on the school bulletin board. Mr. Stevens, the principal, was furious.

"Still," Chessie said, "there's a big noise about this, hoax or not. The school board is afraid the newspapers will find out. Just imagine what they'd do with a story about a teacher talking to extra . . . extratress—you know what I mean!"

"Extraterrestrials," Sphinx said. "Yeah, whatever it was, Mr. Dawson shouldn't have said anything about it. He missed all of his classes last Thursday and then gave this story as an explanation. Mr. Stevens isn't the type to enjoy hearing about close encounters of the third kind."

The gang nodded. At the far end of the playing field the marching band was practicing and the noise mingled with yells from a pickup game of touch football. A shout went up from the spectators as a tall black teenager danced across the goal line, a football tucked under his arm. He turned with a grin and hoisted the ball triumphantly over his head.

The gang stood up to cheer. " 'Fame comes only when deserved,' " said Larry, sitting down. "Longfellow."

There was a chorus of groans. Ever since Larry had been given a book of quotations on his birthday he had insisted on showing how much of it he had memorized. Threats, pleas, and bribes from his friends had all failed.

"Hey, look," said Bobbie, "someone's coming."

The five of them turned toward the street. A young man

2

in a business suit had just gotten out of his car and was walking toward them. A camera was slung around his neck, and he carried a small notebook.

"What's this?" Chessie murmured.

The man walked up to the grandstand and smiled at them. "Hi, kids. My name's Carl Dresser. I'm a reporter for the *Dispatch*, and if you don't mind, I'd like to ask you a couple of questions."

The gang stared at him. So soon? Diggy thought. It sure didn't take the newspapers very long to pick up the story.

The reporter opened his notebook. "The city editor got a call that someone in your school has seen a UFO. Can you tell me anything about it?"

"A UFO?" Bobbie repeated. "Are you kidding?"

"Here?" Larry said.

"Yes, that's right. We're always interested in stories like that. Our readers get very excited by these sightings. Do you mean you haven't heard about it?"

"Nope," Diggy said. "Sorry."

"Any of you others?" the man asked.

Chessie shook her head, her long dark hair swinging. "Nope. Me neither. What kind of a crazy story is that, anyway?"

"Yes, well," said the reporter, closing his notebook, "okay. Maybe I'll ask some other people around here. Thanks anyway, kids."

"Wait a sec," Sphinx said, munching on his sandwich. His words were muffled. "You didn't ask me. I've heard about the UFO."

The other four looked around in surprise while the reporter smiled and opened his notebook. "Great," he said. "What's the story?"

The redheaded boy sat up and pointed to the south, where the arching span of the Walt Whitman Bridge could be seen faintly through the haze.

"It's Wallops Island," Sphinx said.

"Swallop Island?" repeated the man, scribbling.

"Wallops. Down there off the Virginia coast somewhere. The rocket came from there."

"The rocket?"

"Yeah. NASA does it once in a while, sends up a rocket that shoots out a cloud of gas. Then they watch it spread. Even when it's night down here, it's sunny up there, and the gas glows red, blue—all different colors."

"Why would they do that?"

"They're studying the winds at very high altitudes," the boy said. "But if you don't know about it, it really looks like a spaceship coming down to land. One of the students here saw one last week and thought it was a UFO. Pretty dumb."

The reporter shook his head. "What about this teacher, Allen Dawson? Didn't he see this rocket too?"

"Oh, no," Sphinx said, "he was the one who explained it in class. The whole school's talking about it."

Dresser sighed and put the notebook away. "Okay, kids. Guess there's nothing here for me. Wallops Island, huh?" With a wave of the hand he started across the playing field toward the gate.

"Nice going, Sphinx," Diggy said. "I thought you had lost your mind for a minute there."

The tall redhead was starting in on his second sandwich. "Didn't want him to start asking questions around here. He'd have heard the whole thing soon enough." He gazed off at the disappearing figure of the reporter.

The school bell rang. "Listen." Diggy said, "let's meet after classes and have a talk with Mr. Dawson. That's the only way to find out what's really going on."

The others nodded and filed back toward the building.

□

At the end of the day Diggy and Chessie headed straight for the second-floor biology classroom. Sphinx, Bobbie, and Larry were waiting on the landing. The five friends paused outside the door of Mr. Dawson's room and peered through the window.

The young biology teacher was slumped at his desk, his head lowered, his chin propped in his hands. At Sphinx's soft knock he straightened up and turned toward the door. When he saw their faces, he sat back with a wan smile and waved them in.

"Well, hello, all of you. All the Galaxy Gang except Tilo. I missed him today. Where is he?"

"Downtown becoming a citizen," Chessie said. "He was all excited about it."

"Well, that's good." Mr. Dawson's voice was tight and edgy. He stared past them at the door. "Would you mind closing that, Sphinx? I'm not in the mood for many visitors today."

"Mr. Dawson," Diggy said, "we heard some rumor about your seeing . . . ummm . . . a UFO."

The teacher sighed. "Never believe rumors, Diggy. Except for this one, of course."

"Then it's true?" Chessie said. They moved closer around his desk.

"Mr. Dawson," Larry said, "if you don't want to talk about it, we won't bother you. It's just that all these stories are going around, and we wondered what the truth was."

"If we knew, maybe we could help—at least in stopping the rumors," Bobbie said.

Mr. Dawson turned toward the window. He ran a hand through his dark hair, which stood up wildly, and then locked his hands behind his head. He shrugged, with a faint smile. "I don't know what to tell you," he said. "The whole thing's been a nightmare. I don't mind saying that I wouldn't object to having the rumors stopped. They're not helping me."

"What happened?" asked Diggy.

"Sit down," said Mr. Dawson. "I suppose I might as well set the record straight. I'll tell you about it, and then you tell me what *you* think."

They sat in the first row of desks and waited.

Mr. Dawson stared off through the window. "For a long time now," he began, "I've been having a hard time sleeping. I've been watching TV, reading, staring up at the ceiling— but it's been hard to fall asleep. I'd try to get some work down, but I just couldn't concentrate.

"So, lately I've been taking long walks to tire myself out. I'd walk anywhere, for miles and miles. I guess it wasn't the safest thing to do, so late at night, but after being in Vietnam I wasn't too worried about the city streets. A few times the police stopped me to ask me questions. After that I stayed away from Center City and started to walk south, toward the airport. I liked to watch the planes coming in, all those lights. I didn't even recognize most of the neighborhoods I walked through, and I didn't really care. I just wanted to be walking.

"Last Thursday night—Friday morning really—I had been walking for a while when I found myself in some woods. One minute I was on the street, and then I sort of woke up from my thoughts and found I had wandered into a

6

swamp. The ground was moist and slippery, and there was the strong smell of rotting leaves."

There was another pause as Mr. Dawson strained to remember what had happened. "I got panicky," he said. "It was just like the jungles in Vietnam—wet, silent, and dark. Anyway, I wandered through it all night trying to get out."

"All *night*?" echoed Bobbie.

"Well, by the time I realized that I had wandered off the road, I was completely lost. I tried to walk toward the sounds of the airplanes, but I was tired and confused, and they seemed to be coming from all directions. Here I was in the heart of a large city—and I was as lost as if it were the Everglades. I stumbled through the trees for a while, and then just had to sit down. I found a dry spot and decided I'd wait for dawn to find my way back."

Mr. Dawson paused, his gaze far away. "And that's when I saw the lights."

"So you did see something," Diggy said.

Mr. Dawson nodded. "There was something there, I swear it. At first all I saw were these flickering lights through the trees. I got up and stumbled toward them. I had no idea what it was, but I thought perhaps there'd be somebody there who could tell me how to get out of the swamp. Well, I went on for about a hundred yards when suddenly I came out of the trees and found myself slipping down a muddy bank into a stream. I grabbed a tree root and pulled myself back up. I was lying on the wet ground, cursing, when I looked downstream . . . and there it was!"

Chessie was flushed with excitement. "What?" she cried.

"Remember, it was foggy and there was no moon, so I couldn't see it very clearly. It was big and shaped like a cylinder, dark-colored, with two or three blue lights on top. It was half-hidden in the bushes at the edge of the trees so that all I saw was the upper part—but it was huge. The green glow was in front of it, close to the ground. It was flickering and spreading out between the cylinder and the stream."

Sphinx leaned forward. "But you can't be sure that it was coming out of the cylinder, could you?" he asked.

"No, not for sure. But you see, that wasn't all. A moment after I first saw the glowing lights, two . . . I don't know what to call them . . . two figures appeared on the bank and looked down into the stream. I don't know how to tell you this, but they looked as if they were in some kind of space suits. Big bulky things with round helmets. I couldn't see any more than that. All I really saw were their outlines against the green light. They stood there for about ten seconds and then disappeared."

"What happened then?" Bobbie asked.

"I thought I was losing my mind. I lay on the mud for a while, staring. Then I got up and tried to get closer to the thing. The stream was too wide to cross at that point, so I had to move away from it. I crossed about a half-mile upstream and ran back, slipping on the wet ground. I was covered with mud and leaves by that time—I must have looked like an alien myself. But when I reached the place where I had seen the lights—I recognized it because there was a sharp bend in the stream there—I found nothing!"

"Nothing!" All five teenagers blurted out their surprise.

Mr. Dawson shook his head. "No glow, no cylinder, no figures in space suits. It was too dark to see any tracks, and anyway the ground was so spongy they wouldn't have lasted long. I lit a match and looked around, but all I could see was a rut, as if a log had been dragged from the woods to the bank. Nothing else."

"How'd you get out of the swamp?" Chessie asked.

"I spent the next two hours huddled under a tree, shivering. When the sun came up, I started walking to the east and found a narrow track that finally brought me out within sight of the airport. I was still trembling. When I got home, I was so tired I slept most of the day. Missed my classes, in fact."

"So you had to explain to the principal where you were, huh?" Bobbie said.

Mr. Dawson nodded. "I should have made up any other excuse, but I was still in shock, and it didn't occur to me to lie. I guess I wanted to tell someone about it. But I never expected the reaction I got. Not from Mr. Stevens; he was very skeptical but polite. No, it was from a man named Twitchell, the president of the school board. Mr. Stevens telephoned him and he came right over. Well, he came storming into the office, made me repeat the whole story, and sat there glowering and muttering to himself while I did. I caught things like 'nonsense,' 'crazy,' and 'out of your mind.' That really shook me, and by the time I was done, I was stammering and almost incoherent."

"Twitchell?" Diggy asked. "Is he a tall, skinny guy with horn-rimmed glasses and big ears?"

Mr. Dawson nodded. "That's the one. Do you know him?"

"Not really," Chessie said. "He's new on the board, but we've heard that he's a lawyer with a lot of pull down at City Hall. I think he's running for City Council or something. Awfully funny way for a lawyer to act—getting mad before he even heard your story."

"Well, to tell you the truth, he had some reason to be suspicious about my mental state. He knew that I . . . I had a nervous breakdown in Vietnam and was in a hospital for over a year."

"You told us that you were a Ranger," Diggy said. "That was a very dangerous job. How long were you over there?"

"Eighteen months. Most of the time on patrol in the jungles. Booby traps, ambushes, heat, snakes . . . it was rough duty. But I finally broke, and they spent a year talking to me before I stopped screaming at night. Mr. Stevens hired me in spite of that. I thought it was all behind me."

"Mr. Dawson," Sphinx asked, "I'd like to ask you something. Do you believe in UFOs?"

Mr. Dawson shook his head, and leaned forward in his chair. "No, Sphinx, I don't. But I can't deny what I saw, and I know it sounds crazy. I don't believe in UFOs, but I'm afraid I'm starting to see things that aren't there. And Twitchell has called a school board meeting for a week from this Wednesday. What can I tell them? It's too late to hush the whole thing up. And you know, I can't blame them. If I *am* starting to see things, then I really shouldn't be teaching here."

"You're a great teacher, Mr. Dawson," Chessie said. "We don't want to lose you."

Mr. Dawson grinned. "Well, that's good to hear. But I'm still going to have to tell my story to a group of ten conservative lawyers and business executives. What are they going to make of it? What can anyone make of it, for that matter?" He sighed. "I'll never get another job teaching if I'm thrown out of here."

There was an embarrassed silence. Mr. Dawson shook his head. "I really shouldn't be discussing this with you," he said. "It's between the school board and me. There's nothing you can do—although I must admit it makes me feel better to talk."

Sphinx tilted back his chair and gazed out the window. "There was something in that swamp," he said. "The question is, what?"

"Do you remember hearing any noises?" Diggy asked.

"No, nothing in particular. But I was so shocked and confused, I probably wouldn't have heard. Nothing but the sound of birds all around me, and the noise of planes."

"Do you have any idea where all this happened?" Larry asked.

Mr. Dawson shook his head. "All I can remember is the woods . . . and how wet it was. Oh yes, the stream, of course, and how it curved out of sight just where I saw the cylinder and the light. Not much help, I'm afraid, but I've only been living in Philadelphia two months."

They left the classroom ten minutes later with what few words of sympathy and encouragement they could think of. The corridors were empty now. Outside, they stopped and looked up at the cloudless October sky.

"Larry has a quote coming on," Sphinx said. "I can feel it."

"Oh," Larry replied, "I can think of several quotes. 'The green mantle of the standing pool.' That's from *King Lear*. Or maybe you prefer 'A green glow in the deep thicket's gloom.' I think that's by Goethe. But what's bothering me is the 'green glow.' I've heard that somewhere before, and not in a quotation."

They waited while Larry struggled to remember, but finally he shook his head. "No use, it's gone. Maybe it'll come back to me if I don't concentrate too hard."

"Okay," Diggy said, "it's time for a planning session. We'll meet in the park in an hour. I'll call Tilo and get him over there. Can everyone make it?"

They all nodded.

"Good," Diggy said. "This is going to take all our collective brain power. We've got a real puzzler here."

2

☐ The Galaxy Gang met in a small park across the street from Diggy's apartment building. Tilo was there, eager for news about Mr. Dawson. Sphinx, lying on his side and gesturing in the air, told him about the mysterious goings-on in the swamp. Tilo's eyes grew rounder and rounder.

"Do you think it was really a . . . a . . ." the Vietnamese boy faltered.

"UFO?" finished Diggy. He rolled over onto his back and stared at the trees overhead. "No, I don't. I *do* think he saw something—but not aliens with bug eyes and antennae."

Tilo sighed. Since coming to the United States two years ago, he had learned a lot from old detective movies and westerns on TV. Recently Sphinx had introduced him to science fiction, which Tilo now read with a passion. He was disappointed by Diggy's attitude. His adventurous mind rejected any practical explanation of Mr. Dawson's strange story.

Larry laughed. "Tilo's hoping this will turn out to be *Close Encounters of the Third Kind, Part Two*," he teased. "He'd like us all to be spirited off to another galaxy!"

"Great," Chessie said, "then I won't have to finish my French homework."

"And I won't have to worry about this Science Fair project," said Bobbie.

"And I won't have to write any more English essays," said Tilo.

"And I'll never eat pizza again," Sphinx moaned.

"And *I*," said Diggy, "won't have to go to the Naval Academy!"

A short silence greeted this last remark. Diggy lay on his back, staring up at the sky. His friends all knew that Diggy's father was a naval officer and wanted Diggy to apply to Annapolis. He had even urged Diggy to take cram courses on the weekends to prepare for the entrance exam. Diggy had escaped by pleading an overload of regular schoolwork, but he had not told his father that he had no interest in a naval career. Finally Diggy broke the silence, "So, where do we begin?"

Sphinx took a map from the pocket of his jacket and waved it. "It's easy to figure out where Mr. Dawson saw that thing. He went south and was close to the airport. He was in a woods with swampy ground. Only one place it could have been: the bird sanctuary, Tinicum Marsh."

He unrolled the map and pointed to a large green area north of the airport. "See, here it is. And here's the stream running through it—it's called Darby Creek. And right here is where it makes a big curve. That must be the spot."

They inspected the map and nodded their agreement. "What's this?" Chessie asked, pointing to a long black line. Sphinx took a closer look. "That's a boardwalk across the lagoon in the center of the swamp. If you come in from the highway here, the quickest way to the curve in the stream is along that boardwalk."

"Okay," Diggy said. "Now we know where Mr. Dawson was. Can anybody guess what it was he saw?"

"Maybe it was a UFO." Tilo pleaded. "You'd expect it to land at night if they didn't know if we'd be hostile or not."

"And the green light?" Bobbie's voice sounded doubtful.

Tilo had his answer ready. "It could be a gas from their engines. Or maybe it's some way of protecting themselves from intruders—from someone trying to attack them. Or maybe it's their way of testing the air or how strong the ground is."

"Well," Diggy said, "we don't know enough to prove or disprove that. I think we should leave a real UFO as our last guess, after we've tried every other possibility."

Everyone but a crestfallen Tilo murmured their agreement.

"My theory," Sphinx proclaimed, "is called 'Science Teacher Tricked by Glowing Marsh Gas.' You know, marsh gas forms in swamps from the rotting leaves and trees. It can be ignited by lightning or a spark. Lots of people have mistaken it for a UFO." He glanced vaguely around at the group. Sphinx's eyes always looked slightly unfocused while he talked to you, as if his brain was elsewhere, off solving equations and jumping through mathematical hoops. That, combined with his wild red hair and patched jeans, made him look permanently disheveled.

"That's my idea," he said.

"No good," Larry replied, shaking his head. Larry wanted to be an engineer and was always practical. "There hasn't been a storm in this area in weeks. And if the marsh gas was ignited by a spark, why didn't that happen when Mr. Dawson lit the match? And why was it on the ground instead of floating above it?"

Sphinx looked glum. "You've killed my theory," he said, and began to chew on a piece of grass.

"It's not only the lights," Chessie said. "What about that big cylinderlike thing he saw? What could that have been?"

"Maybe it was just a big tree that had fallen down," Bobbie suggested. "You know, it was dark and foggy, and Mr. Dawson couldn't see very well."

"Yeah, but he saw enough to remember that there were blue lights on top of it," Diggy said.

"And he looked over the the area afterwards and didn't say anything about a fallen tree," said Sphinx.

Bobbie sighed in mock despair. "Okay," she admitted, "it couldn't have been a tree."

"How abut the two creatures in space suits?" asked Larry. "Any ideas about that?"

"Sure," Chessie said. "I think that maybe they were large bears. With the darkness and all the fog, they could have been bulky enough to look as though they were wearing space suits."

"Not bad," said Sphinx, still lying on his back, "but unfortunately there haven't been any bears in Tinicum Marsh for over a hundred years."

"Very old bears, then," said Chessie with a laugh.

"Maybe they were deer?" Bobbie suggested.

"Wearing helmets?" Diggy said. He stood up and began to pace nervously. "This is no good. We can go on guessing forever. We're not going to get anywhere this way."

"Well, there's got to be a reasonable explanation," Bobbie said. She stood up, put her arms straight up over her head, and bent slowly backward until her hands touched the ground in a perfect U shape. Upside down, she goggled at Diggy.

"After all," she said sweetly, "weird things like that don't happen—do they?"

"I told you that gymnastics would end up scrambling

your brains," Sphinx said. Bobbie laughed and stood up in one swift, graceful motion.

"Anyway," she said, sitting down in a lotus position, "I don't believe in aliens and all of that."

"Right," Larry said. "Remind me not to take you to the movies when *Star Wars* comes around again."

"Okay, gang," Diggy said, "listen. We're not getting anywhere. I think there's only one way of finding out what happened to Mr. Dawson that night."

"And what's that?" Chessie asked.

"We'll have to go there ourselves, and stay there all night long. If there's anything weird going on there, we might see it too."

There was a silence. The gang members looked at each other. The thought of sitting in Tinicum Marsh for the entire night was not particularly attractive. Bobbie's face lost its look of Buddhalike calm as she glanced around at the others. At last Larry cleared his throat.

"'I have rarely seen courage at two o'clock in the morning,'" he quoted solemnly. "Napoleon Bonaparte."

"I knew I could trust Larry to come up with something," said Sphinx.

"I think Diggy's right," Chessie said. "Seeing for ourselves is the only way."

Tilo was the only one who did not look in the least bit dismayed. His face was glowing.

"It could be fun," he said eagerly.

Larry groaned. "Let Tilo do it, then!"

"Our parents will never let us out so late," Bobbie said. "We'll have to sneak in and out of the house without waking them up."

"We'll be dead in school the next day," mourned Sphinx. "Oh, well," he said, perking up, "I always sleep through English and history, anyway."

"There's one thing," said Diggy. "I don't think we should all go together. If we do, we won't be good for more than one night's watch, and it may take more than that before that thing—whatever it is—shows up again. Also, six of us might attract too much attention getting in and out of the swamp. I think we should split up into three groups of two and go on different nights."

"Good idea," Sphinx said. He looked around. "I choose Tilo. He'll need a steady hand on his shoulder to hold him back if we do see anything. Otherwise he'll just leap forward and beg to be taken along to another planet."

The Vietnamese boy laughed. "Okay, it's a deal."

"Fine," Diggy said. "How about you, Bobbie?"

"Oh, I'll go with Larry. I figure he can bore me with his quotes while we're sitting in the swamp."

"I'll bring my quote book," Larry said ominously.

"That leaves me and Chess," Diggy said. "Can you go tonight?" he asked the dark-haired girl.

Chessie smiled up at him.

"Why, Diggy, an invitation to a swamp! How delightful! *Whatever* shall I wear?"

"Old jeans, a heavy sweater, and a warm coat," said Sphinx. "It's cold at night. And don't forget hiking shoes."

"Right," Diggy said. "I'll be at your house at midnight, Chessie."

"Don't forget," Bobbie reminded them, "we're having dinner with the judge tonight."

□

Judge Thomas Jarrell sat at the head of the table and smiled at his young friends. The judge was thoroughly enjoying this gathering, which was in honor of his birthday. ("Although at seventy-two, perhaps I should stop celebrating the passage of the years," he had said jovially. Between spoonfuls of sherbet and chocolate cake the Galaxy Gang had protested loudly that the judge looked and acted like a much younger man.) Mrs. Emily, the judge's longtime housekeeper and cook, laughed at the group's high spirits and beamed at the sight of the empty plates that covered the table.

"Well now," the judge asked, "what have you been up to lately? And I might add that I'm almost afraid to ask."

His guests grinned. Only a month ago the judge had kept them out of a great deal of trouble in what they now called "The Computer Caper." That was a scheme that had saved Tilo's parents from being cheated of their savings and had exposed a swindler named Baring, but it was only by a hairsbreadth that the gang had avoided breaking the law.

"Nothing to worry you, Your Honor," Chessie said. "Right now we're into UFOs."

The judge nodded. "Yes, I've read the newspapers. Some sort of hysteria going around about these sightings. A lot of nonsense."

"One of our teachers saw one," Sphinx said between sips of hot chocolate.

Their host frowned and put down his cup. "I suppose a teacher is no more immune to these optical illusions than a truckdriver or a politician."

"You don't believe there's anything in these UFO reports, judge?" Larry's voice was excited. Judge Jarrell shook his head.

Larry took a newspaper clipping from his jacket pocket. "This was in the *Dispatch* about a week ago. It seems that the pilot of a charter plane coming into Philadelphia International Airport looked down through a break in the clouds while he was on his final approach. He saw a patch of mysterious flickering light, which he described, and I quote, as 'a pool of moving light with a greenish glow.'"

The judge did not catch the quick, knowing glances that Larry's friends exchanged. "What time did all this happen?" he asked.

"About two o'clock in the morning," Larry replied.

"So," the judge said with a satisfied air, "we have a pilot tired after a long flight. He looks down through a break in the clouds and sees what? The reflection of his own wingtip light? The lights of a parking lot? It could be a dozen things. And the motion of his plane makes him think the lights are moving. No, my boy, you can't get me to believe in UFOs with evidence like that."

"Tell me, judge," Diggy said, "do you know a man named Twitchell, the president of our school board?"

The older man thought for a moment. "I seem to recall the name. Is he a lawyer?" Diggy nodded. "Oh, yes, I remember now. He represented a corporation in a case that came up before me about five or six years ago. Tried to use political pressure on me—I got a few calls from City Hall about the matter. Soon put an end to that. Why do you ask?"

"He doesn't believe in UFOs either," Diggy said innocently.

"Well, Diggy, if you look hard enough, I'm certain that you'll find plenty of lawyers who believe the aliens have landed—and even more who suspect that some of the bug-eyed monsters have been elected judges!"

The gang helped Mrs. Emily clear the table, then presented the judge with his birthday present. It was an oak walking stick with a carved lion's head, wrapped in a knitted sleeve and locked in a black leather case. Both the judge and his housekeeper exclaimed over the beautiful workmanship.

"We all made it, judge, but you'll never guess who did what," Chessie said.

"Please tell me," Judge Jarrell said. "I'd like to thank each one of you."

"Well," Chessie said with a slight smile, "I turned the stick on a lathe in the school shop."

"And I carved the lion's head," Bobbie said proudly.

"Diggy and I made the case," Larry put in.

"And I knitted the sleeve," Sphinx said. "Knit one, purl two, and drop three."

The gang left shortly after that, with the judge's thanks still ringing in their ears. Since tomorrow was a school day, no one expected them to linger, but in the back of their minds was the knowledge that Chessie and Diggy would be spending the night in the depths of the swamp.

□

The two teenagers sat quietly on the airport bus. Diggy stared out the window as the bus droned southward on the deserted street. Next to him, Chessie huddled in her jacket, her eyes wide. Neither wanted to speak. They could not help wondering what was waiting for them in Tinicum Marsh.

It had been easy to sneak out of the house, Chessie thought. Her parents were used to her escapades, but there hadn't been any in a while, and so they weren't as alert as usual. They had bid her a cheerful good night as she went up to bed. She had dutifully turned out her light a short while later, only to sit on her bed, fully dressed, waiting. At 11:30, after the evening news, she heard the door of her parents' bedroom close, and half an hour later she slipped down the stairs and out of the house by the back door. Diggy had been waiting as promised. They had walked the few short blocks to the airport bus. Now here they were, speeding south. Why were they doing this, anyway?

Diggy stared out the window. He knew that what they were doing could be dangerous. There was no telling what that object Mr. Dawson had seen really was. Glowing lights and men in space suits did not add to his sense of confidence. But he could not think of any other way to solve the mystery. Whatever it was, whoever was involved, could not possibly suspect that anyone would be watching. Not in a swamp in the dead of night.

He took out the large map of the city which Larry had given to him and studied it one more time. He traced the route from the bus stop near the bird sanctuary to the stream which ran through the swamp. They would have to head northwest to hit the stream. He had brought along a compass and a flashlight as well.

"Diggy, c'mon! This is our stop," Chessie whispered, getting to her feet.

The bus driver stared at them as they scrambled down the steps. "I don't like the idea of you kids getting off here this late," he grumbled. "You're sure your teacher is meeting you here?"

"Oh, yes," Diggy replied. "It's a field trip, like I told you. Our teacher is very interested in nocturnal birds."

The bus driver shrugged. The door closed behind them, and the two teenagers found themselves alone on a deserted road. There, in front of them, was the entrance to Tinicum Marsh.

Diggy took out the compass and the flashlight. He looked at the map one last time, then folded it and put it in his jacket pocket.

"Okay, Chess," he said, "let's go!"

□

It took them a long time, stumbling through the underbrush, their feet squelching on the soft ground, before they finally found the stream. According to the map, it ran straight for a while before it widened and made a sharp curve. That was the place they were looking for. They followed the muddy banks for about a quarter of an hour, slipping and sliding on the wet ground. Suddenly Diggy put up a hand and pointed.

"There," he said in a low voice, "can you see it?"

Chessie peered into the darkness. In front of them the black waters widened into a large pond before the stream curved sharply out of sight. It was just as Mr. Dawson had described it.

"Thank goodness," she whispered. "I couldn't have walked much longer. Let's find someplace to sit down."

They found a small patch of dry earth under a tree and sat down, huddling together. It was very dark. The moon was just a sliver in the sky, seen faintly through the drifting clouds. It was cold and Chessie shivered in her jacket. Diggy shone his flashlight on his watch: five minutes after two.

"Chessie," he whispered, "Mr. Dawson said he saw the—whatever it was—about two hours before dawn. That would make it around three or three-thirty. If we don't see anything by then, and you're really cold, we'll just leave, okay?"

"No," said the girl, "We said we'd stay all night, and we will. I have to be back home before my parents get up, so we should leave here around five o'clock. It'll be almost light by then."

"Okay," Diggy said. He shifted his position on the cold ground. Overhead there came the low ghostly hoot of an owl, and both of them jumped. There was a flutter of wings, a low scrabbling sound in the bushes, and then a tiny squeak, which was suddenly cut off. They heard a rustling, then all was silent.

"Owl got a mouse," whispered Diggy.

"Wonderful," said Chessie. Her hands were shaking. "I forgot this was a bird sanctuary. This place is filled with unidentified flying objects." There was a pause, then she added thoughtfully, "Poor mouse."

"I'm hungry," Diggy said.

"I can't believe that you can eat after that," said the girl. She reached into her knapsack and brought out two sandwiches wrapped in tinfoil. "Here. Ham and cheese, or ham and cheese?"

"I'll take this one."

"Okay."

They sat together, quietly munching, their eyes wide in the darkness. All was quiet around them. One of them was always watching the place where the stream curved. It was there, on the far bank, that Mr. Dawson had seen the glowing cylinder and the mysterious helmeted figures. Now they saw nothing but the stream and the dark shapes of trees and shrubs on the banks. Occasionally there was a *plop!* in the lake as a fish jumped. The bushes around them rustled as the swamp animals went about their nightly business. Chessie grew sleepier and sleepier and took short naps on Diggy's shoulder. The boy sat quietly, his head nodding now and then as fatigue swept over him. But one of them was awake, watching, as the other slept. They saw nothing. The bird sanctuary stretched out on all sides of them, tranquil in the darkness.

□

It was 5:30 A.M. when two stiff, muddy, exhausted figures stumbled out of Tinicum Marsh and walked down the street to the bus stop. Chessie was thinking of a long, steaming hot bath, and Diggy was thinking of his bed. Half an hour later the bus finally picked them up. The driver and passengers stared as they climbed up the steps and collapsed on a seat.

"My eyelids aren't working," sighed Chessie.

"Will you look at these," Diggy said glumly, lifting his mud-caked shoes. "I'll never get them clean."

"Diggy," said the girl, "do you think we waited at the wrong spot? There was nothing there—nothing!"

With a groan Diggy let his head fall back against the seat.

"No," he said. He groped for the map and opened it. "There's no other place where the stream widens and then curves like that. We were where Mr. Dawson was, Chess."

"We just weren't as lucky as he was," Chessie snapped back. "Why couldn't he have gone there last night, instead of last week? He wouldn't have seen a thing and we wouldn't be in this mess!"

"Right. Then we could've gotten some sleep last night," Diggy moaned. He sat with his head back and his eyes closed. Then he grinned and turned to the girl.

"Anyway, Chess," he said, "*we* may be the lucky ones."

"Why?"

"Because we get to sleep tonight," Diggy said, "and Larry and Bobbie have to go sit in that swamp!"

3

□ "Nothing," Bobbie yawned. "We saw absolutely nothing." She put her head down on the table and closed her eyes.

Larry sat back and groaned. It was Wednesday morning. His tired voice could hardly be heard above the noisy chatter in the school lunchroom. The rest of the gang leaned forward to listen.

"We got there about two A.M. and found the spot without much trouble. . ."

"Except that I slipped and slid down a muddy bank almost into the water," complained Bobbie.

"Well, it was hard to see where we were going. There was some fog, and it was a cloudy night anyway. We huddled under a blanket and watched the bend in the stream. We could hear animals moving around in the bushes and some plane noises, but nothing else. It was really spooky."

"Larry didn't even come up with any good quotes," Bobbie said.

"I was too tired."

"Didn't you see anything?" Chessie asked.

"Nope," Larry said. "Zilch. Zero. Nothing moved in that swamp all night long, except for the two of us shivering. The only human noise I heard was Bobbie complaining. As soon as it started to get light, we left."

"My mother almost caught me sneaking in," Bobbie said. "She was in the kitchen making breakfast. I forgot my father was catching an early plane. I went around to the back and up the stairs—I was more scared of her finding out than I was of sitting in that swamp. I hid my clothes in the back of the closet. With my luck, she'll decide that today is laundry day and go snooping around in my room."

There was a long silence as the gang munched on their sandwiches. Two days now and nothing to report. The school board was going to meet a week from today. What if they had come up with nothing by then? What if Mr. Dawson really had been seeing things?

"I don't believe it," Chessie said, answering their unspoken thoughts. "Do you?"

"No," Diggy said, tilting back his chair. "No, I don't either, Chess."

"We still have tonight," Tilo said. "Maybe Sphinx and I will see it."

"What worries me is that Mr. Dawson may have frightened off whatever it was," Bobbie said. "You know, maybe it saw him and won't be back."

"But he said he wasn't anywhere near the spot until after it was gone," Sphinx objected. "And it was dark, with the fog and everything. It's not too likely he was spotted."

"Maybe they heard him. He was stumbling around, he says. Maybe that thing heard him and took off," Bobbie replied.

They finished their lunch in gloomy silence.

"Larry," said Sphinx, when the bell rang, "are you going to be around tonight before dinner?"

"Yeah, I'll be at home. Why?"

"Oh, I have an idea about something. I'd like to come by and borrow some stuff from you."

Larry shrugged. "Okay, be mysterious. Come by around five."

28

"Thanks." Sphinx got to his feet. "I'm going to go visit Professor Larsen after school today, so I'll be over after that."

"You're just full of ideas," teased Chessie.

Sphinx smiled, strolling away. "Wish Tilo and me luck tonight. We'll need it!"

□

"The most interesting thing," the professor was saying, "is not the sightings themselves—we can usually explain those—but why people want to believe in them."

He was a short, plump man of about forty. He sat back in his leather armchair and smiled across the desk at the redheaded boy. Sphinx and he had met at the Science Fair two years ago and had been friends ever since. They usually talked about Sphinx's projects and Professor Larsen's field of interest, clinical psychology.

"Most of the sightings can be explained?" Sphinx asked.

"Oh, yes. Unusual cloud formations, distant lights, balloons, aircraft lights, marsh gas, mirages . . . all these have been mistaken for UFOs. Particularly if the light is poor and they only appear briefly. People will reject commonsense explanations in favor of wild stories about aliens, spaceships, and so on. It has to do with wanting to be special, I think."

"But, professor, there are some unexplained sightings and even some photographs of these objects."

"Well, yes, I believe there are, but that only means we haven't found the answer to them yet, Sphinx. They are probably just ordinary objects seen under extraordinary conditions."

"And those stories about people who have talked with aliens and been taken away in their spaceships?"

The professor laughed. "I believe it's nonsense, Sphinx. People who want to be noticed, be different—people who want to give up responsibility for their lives and be guided by a superior alien intelligence—these are the kind of people who see UFOs and take trips into outer space. Some people are honestly bewildered by what seems to be a very strange sight, of course—but many sightings are reported by people who just want to believe that they've seen something different."

Sphinx thought this over. "Would a bad experience, really frightening, maybe a series of them over a few months, make a man more likely to see things?"

"Of course. The mind is a very fragile vessel."

"Would long periods of sleeplessness do the same thing?"

"Again, yes. Fatigue can affect all your senses and give you false signals."

"So a UFO sighting wouldn't be unusual for someone who had been under stress and couldn't sleep?"

"That's right. He might even welcome the idea, to divert him from his own painful feelings."

"Or to get him out of a situation he didn't like—a job, say?"

Professor Larsen paused. "Hmmm, yes. If he wanted to quit, but couldn't take the responsibility for it, he might manufacture an experience which would force him out of it."

Sphinx sighed and stood up. "Thanks, professor."

"Anything else I can tell you before you go, Sphinx?"

"Well, I do have one more thing I wanted to ask you. Do you think you could let me have a roll of that infrared film you were telling me about? I'd like to take some pictures in the dark."

The professor reached inside a desk drawer and handed over a small roll of film. "Here you are. I don't need any more, so use it all up if you want. I think I can get the photo lab here at the university to develop the prints for you afterwards. Is this for a new experiment?"

"Well, sort of." The boy shoved the film into his pocket and smiled. "What would you say if I told you I was going to try and photograph a UFO?"

The professor looked at him. "I'd say you'd better sit back down and we'll talk about it."

"No time," Sphinx said cheerfully. "I've got to run. Thanks a lot, professor!"

□

"I don't get it," Larry protested. "What do you want all this stuff for? Either you see it or you don't. Either you hear something or you don't. Why lug a camera and tape recorder along?"

Sphinx stuffed the miniature tape recorder into his jacket pocket, ran the wire up his sleeve, and taped the tiny microphone to his right index finger. He pointed at the window of Larry's bedroom and squeezed his arm against the pocket. He could hear the low hum of the tape recorder as it clicked on. He grinned, satisfied.

"The pressure switch works fine. Thanks, Larry. Now all I have to do is point, squeeze, and I'll have the sound on tape. If there is one, of course."

"Of course."

"Well, I can't believe that something that big could just vanish without a sound. Now see, when I reach for the camera, I'll be squeezing this pocket at the same time. If it disappears before I can get a picture, maybe there'll be something on the tape."

"Oh, there'll be something on the tape all right," Larry said. "Your heavy breathing and Tilo's screams. That ought to sound great."

Sphinx refused to be provoked. "How long will the batteries last?"

"Long enough. They're fresh. They'll last two or three hours even if you run them constantly."

There was a knock on the door. "Okay, I'm coming. Be right down," Larry shouted. He turned back to Sphinx. "Good luck, okay? I'll think of you two as I go to sleep in my nice warm bed tonight."

"And you can be sure Tilo and I will be thinking about you and the others while we're freezing out in that swamp."

"Yeah, well," Larry said, opening the door, "if there *is* anything out there, it doesn't stand a chance against you and all your equipment. Good luck!"

□

In his small room above the tailor shop Tilo lay in bed and stared up at the ceiling. The lights of passing cars rippled across the walls, forming strange patterns.

A distant church bell rang the quarter hour. Twelve fifteen. It was time to go. He got up and dressed, quickly and silently. As he struggled into the heavy clothes he wondered whether he was dressed too warmly, but he hated the cold. He was still not used to the bitter winters here.

Groping his way down the stairs in the dark, he felt for the back door. He eased it open, pausing to listen for any sounds behind him. No, the whole family was fast asleep. He waited for a moment, then slipped out the door and closed it quietly.

The bus stop was three blocks away. As Tilo turned the corner he saw Sphinx leaning against the signpost, his jacket wrapped tightly around him.

"Hi," the redhead said.

"Hi."

Sphinx was holding a paper bag. "Brought some food for both of us," he said. "I get hungry if I'm awake for more than two hours."

"Thanks." They shivered on the corner for fifteen minutes before the airport bus arrived. There were only three other passengers. Sphinx and Tilo sat near the back, slumped in their seats.

The ride took twenty minutes. As the two teenagers clambered off the bus the driver leaned down and said, "Listen, I don't know what's going on here, but I'm telling you, if I see any more of you kids on this bus at one in the morning, I'm going to call the cops." The doors closed and the bus moved on.

"Great," said Sphinx, watching it. "We're going to be arrested for riding a city bus."

They crossed the street and plunged into the swamp. They had gone no more than about fifty yards when the streetlights were gone and they were surrounded by woods. Sphinx went first, with Tilo right on his heels, both of them glancing around nervously.

They pushed their way through the brush and thickets. Once an animal—it looked like a raccoon—ran right in front of them. Sphinx stopped so suddenly that Tilo bumped into him.

"Tilo," the redhead whispered, "you're climbing up my back. Watch it." He checked Diggy's compass again and set off at a quicker pace.

It was almost two when they stumbled on the stream. For the last forty minutes they had slipped and slithered on the spongy ground. Once Tilo stumbled and fell, and Sphinx had to go back and help him up. Their shoes were soaked, and Tilo was covered with mud.

"There's the stream," said Sphinx, breathing hard. "Thank goodness. Okay, this way."

They followed the dark waters for almost a quarter of a mile. Tilo grabbed Sphinx's arm and pointed. "There! The curve in the stream. You see it?"

Sphinx peered. "You sure, Tilo? I can't see a thing."

"I'm sure. You city people are blind in the dark, you know that?"

"Are you kidding? I can spot a mugger at fifty yards. Now, where is it?"

They struggled on a little farther, then Sphinx halted. "Okay, right you are. Let's find a place to sit down." They spread a ground sheet underneath a tree and sat back to back, pressing against each other for warmth. Sphinx wanted both of them to watch the length of the stream, in case anything showed up in another spot. They switched positions every quarter hour to ease their cramped legs. Around three o'clock the wind died, and fog began to form close to the ground. The curve in the stream was veiled in a faint white shroud. Once or twice they heard the whine of jet engines or the shrill cry of a bird.

Around four they unwrapped the cheese sandwiches and began to eat. It seemed so pointless. Why would the thing appear tonight, and not last night or the one before? The professor's words ran through Sphinx's mind. *Fatigue can affect all your senses and give you false signals . . .* I guess that's true for me too, he thought.

He glanced over at the curve in the stream. His eyelids

began to droop. His head nodded, and he groaned to himself. This was torture.

Suddenly he felt a hand on his shoulder.

"Wha . . . ?" he gasped, sitting up with a jerk.

Tilo was shaking him. *"Look!"*

Sphinx twisted around and stared. In the distance the trees suddenly stood out clearly, outlined by a flickering green light!

4

☐   Sphinx had expected Tilo to scream, choke, or freeze in terror; he had feared the worst from his overheated imagination. Instead, Sphinx found himself sitting, his mouth open, while the slender Vietnamese boy rose to a half-crouch and moved, swiftly and silently, in the direction of the flickering green light.

"Come *on!*" Tilo whispered.

Sphinx sat dumbfounded. Then he shook his head, clambered to his feet, and went after Tilo.

As they drew closer the two boys could see the stream more clearly. The weird sheet of green light was dancing close to the ground, almost up to the bank. And there, on the other side of the stream, was something that looked . . . like a large cylinder! It was half-hidden in the trees and bushes, and its outlines were dim through the fog, but they could see something big and curved. And standing next to it, on the bank, were . . .

"Aliens!" Tilo gasped. His thin body shook with excitement.

"Sssshh," Sphinx hissed, fumbling for his camera.

They were still some distance away, but the figures were clear enough. There, lit by the greenish glow, were two creatures in space suits. They were standing motionless, staring down into Darby Creek. They were wearing heavy, bulky suits, topped with round metal-and-glass bubbles.

Tilo, beside himself with delight, slipped through the

bushes. Sphinx stumbled behind him, his feet slipping in the mud, his face scratched by sharp branches. He had his camera out and now was frantically trying to focus it. He pressed his arm against his side, and the faint *whirr* from his pocket told him the tape recorder was on. As he hastily snapped a picture he thought he heard a strange grinding sound coming from the cylinder. He stopped and pointed his finger towards the sound, then took a few more shots.

Tilo had vanished. As Sphinx ducked into the bushes to find him, the greenish glow died, and he was left in complete darkness. He scrambled through the mud and branches, seized by a sudden panic: what if they had found Tilo? What if they had spirited him away in that cylindrical thing? What if they had hurt him? *Where could he be?*

"Tilo!" he called, struggling toward the stream. "*Tilo!*"

"I'm here," said a voice on his right, and Tilo appeared out of the fog and darkness.

Sphinx stared, breathing heavily. "Listen, Tilo," he said, "I'm really glad I was here to calm you down. You almost gave me a heart attack."

"Did you see it?" cried the other boy. "Did you see it? I was really close when the green light went out. That—that thing in the bushes . . . and the two aliens in space suits . . . and the light . . . it's all just the way Mr. Dawson described it!"

Sphinx nodded and patted his camera.

"I got some pictures," he said, "and a recording of the sound it made. Let's hope they turn out."

Tilo was nearly dancing with excitement. "I can't wait to tell the others!" he crowed. "We *saw* it!"

"Yeah." Sphinx leaned over and disentangled his jacket from a thornbush. "You know, Tilo, for some reason I feel like I got the short end of it this time. I'm hungry, and my feet are freezing off. C'mon, let's go find that bus."

□

They climbed on the bus, and Sphinx nodded to the driver. It was six A.M.

"Amazing birds," Sphinx said cheerfully. "Amazing, what you can see in that swamp. All kinds of wildlife. A real treat for a birdwatcher."

The driver grunted. The doors swung shut, and the bus rumbled off down the road. Collapsed on one of the seats, the two boys looked at each other and smiled.

□

"Well," said Larry, "at least you got something. I was sure all we'd hear were birdcalls."

It was lunchtime, and the gang had gathered in an empty classroom to listen to the tape.

Sphinx shook his head. "But what is it?" he asked. "Doesn't sound like anything to me."

They were listening for the fifth time to the short sequence of groaning, grinding metallic sounds that Sphinx had recorded. There were also the clicks of the camera and, at the end, the whine of a jet plane overhead.

Diggy bit into his sandwich. As he chewed he tried to picture the scene on the bank of the stream as Tilo and Sphinx had described it.

"I think it's safe to assume," he said between mouthfuls, "that the sound—whatever it is—was coming from the cylinder. Agreed?" They all nodded.

"No other place it could be from," Sphinx said. "Unless

maybe it's the sound of those two spacemen grinding their teeth."

Diggy looked around at the gang. "If they've got teeth and jaws that strong, we'd better not tangle with them."

"The light seemed to be coming from the cylinder," Tilo put in. "Like the sound."

"Except that the light was there all the time and the sound only lasted about five seconds," Sphinx said.

There was a silence.

"Well," said Diggy, "we'll just have to wait and see what's on the film. When will you have it, Sphinx?"

Sphinx stretched out his legs and yawned.

"Right after school today," he said, "I'm going over to the university to get it developed in the professor's lab. Of course," he added accusingly, "I would *much rather* go home and get some sleep . . . but in the interests of science, et cetera, et cetera . . . I don't know how long it will take to get prints."

"I'll go with you, Sphinx," Tilo offered.

The redhead looked over at him. "Okay, Tilo. Thanks. You can shake me if I fall asleep."

"Fine," Diggy said. "We'll meet at lunch tomorrow for the first showing of the new UFO film—if it's ready by then."

□

Sphinx and Tilo came into the cafeteria the next day, sat down with the rest of the gang, and said nothing. Tilo's face was blank, and Sphinx seemed worried and concerned about something. He held a manila folder clutched in his hand.

"Okay, guys," Larry said. "What is it?"

"You found something on the film, right?" Bobbie asked.

"C'mon, tell us," Chessie said.

"I can tell they're going to torture us with it," Diggy complained, waving his sandwich indignantly.

Tilo and Sphinx sat perfectly still.

"It's something on the film," said Larry.

"I know what it is," Chessie said. "Two spacemen holding a large sign saying, We Are Aliens from Outer Space."

"The first real proof that UFOs actually do exist!" Diggy said, laughing.

"Cabbage people from the planet Jupiter," Bobbie suggested.

Tilo cleared his throat and said, "You tell them, Sphinx."

Sphinx took three photographs from the folder and threw them on the table. "Nothing, absolutely nothing. I struck out."

There was a stunned silence. They examined the photographs carefully, hoping that Sphinx was wrong. All they could see were swirls of light and dark. There was one large light blob with fuzzy edges almost in the center of the picture, but of the green glow and the cylinder there was no trace.

"What happened?" Diggy asked.

Sphinx threw up his hands. "I can't figure it out. I had plenty of time to set the camera correctly before we spotted that thing. The fog and the dark don't matter—this is infrared film. It should pick up anything that's giving off heat. Maybe the green light and the cylinder are just plain cold."

"Well," Bobbie said, "this won't convince anyone that Mr. Dawson wasn't dreaming."

"No," Chessie admitted, "and neither will the tape. All we have is the fact that Tilo and Sphinx saw something in the swamp, and you know what the board's going to say about that."

"Yeah, we know," Diggy added. "They'll say that a bunch of kids made this all up to help one of their teachers. 'Nice try, kids, but we don't buy it.'"

Larry groaned and slapped his forehead. "All that sloshing around in the swamp all night, and we've got nothing to show for it. We're right back at square one."

"Wait a minute," Diggy protested, "that's not true. We know that Tilo and Sphinx saw that thing. We can't prove it yet, but we know that Mr. Dawson isn't crazy. Admit it— before this we weren't sure about him."

"That won't convince the school board," Chessie said. "Can you imagine what Twitchell would make of our story?"

Depressed and disappointed, they sat around the cafeteria table searching for a solution to their problem. No one had much of an appetite.

"We could go back to the swamp and lasso the UFO," Tilo said timidly. A chorus of groans and "No, not again" greeted this suggestion.

"Not enough time," Diggy said. "It took us three days to spot it the first time. Who knows how long before it appears again? Today's Friday. The school board meets on Wednesday. Unless we come up with real proof before then, it's all over for Mr. Dawson."

By the time the bell rang, no one had come up with a good idea. Chessie stood up and smoothed her skirt. "I have to go. Next period I'm helping with the invitations to the PTA meeting. See you."

They all left the cafeteria in a gloomy mood. Short of a miracle, nothing could save Mr. Dawson now.

□

Chessie stopped addressing envelopes and looked up at the sound of an angry voice. Coming into the principal's office was Mr. Stevens, looking harassed and upset. Right behind him and almost shouting into his ear was a tall, thin man with jutting ears: Twitchell. The president of the school board did not bother to lower his voice as he followed the principal across the office.

"And we'll have no nonsense about procedure either, Stevens. The whole business is clear. No one in his right mind sees flying saucers, and those who do see them are not fit to teach in this or any other school. I want him dismissed on Wednesday, and I want these rumors squelched before the newspapers get hold of them."

Mr. Stevens stammered a few protests about fairness and the accused's right to be heard, but Twitchell brushed them aside.

"By Wednesday—no later. I would've called this meeting sooner if I could've gotten everyone together. Now I have to make an important private call in your office. See that I'm not disturbed."

Twitchell went into the principal's inner office and slammed the door. Mr. Stevens stared after him for a moment, looked helplessly toward Chessie, then shrugged his shoulders and went into his assistant's office. Chessie felt sorry for Mr. Stevens—Twitchell didn't seem to be the type to keep things quiet and confidential. She turned and stared at the closed door of the principal's office. What was this "important private call" that Twitchell was making?

Another girl was working at a desk on the other side of the outer office. Chessie picked up a pile of envelopes and casually walked over to the file cabinet where the address list was kept. She opened a drawer and flipped slowly through the folders. If anyone had been watching, they would have wondered about the way Chessie's head was cocked to one side and how close her ear was to the principal's door.

It was a thick, heavy door, but Chessie could hear isolated snatches of Twitchell's side of the conversation. His voice was high-pitched and excited, and he seemed to be warning someone about something: "You've got to stop . . . I've got it under control . . . wait until I. . . ." Then he seemed to beg for more time. Whoever he was talking to was making some sort of demand, and Twitchell was frightened. "I'm doing my best for Pluto . . . it's very touchy." This was followed by the sound of the telephone being slammed into its cradle.

By the time a red-faced Twitchell came out of the office, Chessie was back at her desk, absorbed in checking the address list. She did not look up as the board president hurriedly left the room.

She looked up a number in the telephone directory and dialed it. Mrs. Emily answered and brought the judge to the phone. "Your Honor," Chessie said in a whisper, "this is Francesca Morelli. I have a question: what was the name of the company that Mr. Twitchell represented in your court?"

It took the judge a little while to remember the details of a five-year-old case. He went to his files and came back. "Oh, yes, Chessie, it was Pluto Research. I believe they make things for NASA and the Air Force—" Chessie's heart jumped, and she gasped. "What is it, my dear? Are you all right?"

"Yes, sir, I'm fine. You were saying?"

"Chessie, can you tell me what this is all about? I don't want to pry, but I know that when the Galaxy Gang starts to act mysterious—"

"No fear, Your Honor. We've learned our lesson. Good-bye."

Chessie hung up before the judge had a chance to ask why she was suddenly so interested in one of his old cases. She waited impatiently for the bell; her next class was English, and both Diggy and Bobbie would be there.

□

Chessie joined her friends in the back of the classroom and quickly told them the exciting news: Twitchell was tied in with a company that was involved with space research! "Don't you see?" she pleaded. "It's got to be them. Maybe they've made a new secret rocketship, and they're testing it at night. Maybe NASA or the Air Force has captured a UFO and turned it over to Pluto for examination. . ."

"In Tinicum Marsh, in the middle of the night?" Bobbie asked. "How did they get it there?"

"Flew it, of course, to see how it works. Remember the unexplained radar blips?"

"Wait a minute, Chess," Diggy said. "Let's not go too fast. All we know is that the president of our school board is trying hard to get Mr. Dawson fired, and that this has something to do with a research company that he's the lawyer for. It's not much, but it's the best lead we have."

"What do we do now?" Chessie asked.

"Well, after class I'll go find Sphinx, Larry, and Tilo. The library should have a business directory that'll give us the location of Pluto Research. Gosh, Chessie, was that a long distance call?"

"You mean Twitchell's? No, I don't think so. At least I didn't hear him talking to an operator. Of course, he could have dialed it direct."

"Let's hope it's someplace close. I'd like to get a look at what's going on in Pluto Research."

□

It took Diggy and Sphinx less than ten minutes to find that Pluto Research was located in Essington, on the Delaware River not two miles from Tinicum Marsh. "That can't be a coincidence," Sphinx said. "Too many things are falling into place. I think that tomorrow night the Galaxy Gang ought to go take a look at this place. I've always wanted to see a real UFO."

5

☐ "Tilo can't make it," Larry said. "His parents went out, and he's stuck baby-sitting for his brother. He was upset about it, but I told him not to worry. We'll just be looking the place over."

It was Saturday night. The gang had met after dinner on a street corner near Diggy's apartment building. Larry had a city map of Essington with the location of the Pluto Research Company circled in red. "It's right on the river," he said, "next to that marine terminal where all the big ships unload."

Sphinx took a sheet of paper from his pocket. "The Pluto Company manufactures a lot of plastic parts for spacecraft. It has a good credit rating, so it's no fly-by-night operation. The main office and plant are in Essington. I got all this out of a directory in the library. Always good to know who we're dealing with."

The bus came five minutes later, and they filed on in silence. During the ride they sat without talking, staring out at the dark buildings that sped by. There was no plan. They did not even know what they were looking for, except that it glowed in the dark. Why all the mysterious comings and goings in Tinicum Swamp?

The bus let them off in front of a dilapidated warehouse with barred windows and a large metal door.

"If the Pluto building is anything like that," Larry muttered, "we'll never get in."

"Actually," Sphinx said, "we don't really have to get in—if we're lucky. Maybe we can spot this thing from the outside and take a picture of it. Then we'll have everything we need to know."

"A lot of ifs," said Diggy. "C'mon." They buttoned up their jackets against the chilly wind and started walking. After a few blocks they turned a corner and saw a high wire fence with a sign that said, Pluto Research Company. Keep Out. The fence ran across a wide street, which was split by the double tracks of a railroad. Farther down, inside the plant, there was a dimly lit guard box. As they watched, a man in uniform came out of it and began walking toward them along the fence.

"Back!" Chessie whispered.

They shrank into the shadows and froze until the guard had passed them and vanished around a corner of one of the four large buildings inside the fence. Although there were a few lights on high poles scattered throughout the grounds, most of the area was dark. The gang strained their eyes, but there was little to be seen.

"Any ideas where the UFO—or whatever—might be?" asked Diggy.

"It can't be near this street," Sphinx whispered. "The gate next to the guardhouse isn't big enough for it to fly through."

"Very funny," Diggy said. "Okay. One by one. Larry, you go first. Cross the street and wait for us. Watch out for the guards."

Larry nodded and slipped out of the shadows, running across the street and disappearing into the high weeds next to the fence. The other teenagers followed. Bent double and keeping to the shadows where they could, they made their way carefully through the weeds. Fifty yards from their starting point the fence made a right angle.

Larry paused to sniff the air. There was the sharp, salty smell of the river, and in the distance they saw the topmast lights of an invisible ship. The clouds that covered the moon were beginning to break, and they could see the end of the fence, a pier, and a low, squat pump house. Still no sign of a guard.

Suddenly Larry held up an arm and motioned for them to lie down. Holding their breath, they pressed their faces to the damp earth and lay still. There was a rumbling sound, then headlights flashed across their hiding place as a tank truck came up from the pier. It seemed to be headed directly toward them!

"Oh, no!" Diggy muttered.

At the last moment the tanker turned to one side. The fence swung open just ahead of the spot where the gang lay hidden, and the truck moved slowly through and vanished into the plant.

"That was close," Sphinx whispered.

"Through the gate before it closes!" Diggy said, clambering to his feet. They sprinted toward the gate, looking fearfully around as they ran, but there was no warning shout, no pursuit. They slipped through the entrance and huddled behind a low wooden building.

Behind them the gate slowly closed with a loud clanking sound.

"We're in," Bobbie muttered. "Let's hope we get out as easily."

"Okay," said Diggy. "Any ideas on where to look for whatever that UFO might be?"

The gang looked around. There was nothing to be seen but the black, forbidding walls of the various buildings. Not a light showed in any of the windows.

"Let's follow that truck," suggested Sphinx. "I think we should go farther back inside the plant, anyway."

"Yeah, but which way did the truck go?" Larry asked.

"I think it went down this street," Bobbie said, pointing.

Diggy paused, glancing around. "Okay, gang. Listen. If we get separated, we'll meet right back here, next to this building by the gate. Understood?" They nodded. "All right," he said. "Let's go."

In the distance a ship's whistle moaned, a faint, dismal sound. In single file, Larry first and Sphinx bringing up the rear, they crept down the dark street. It was eerie and unreal. The only sound was the shuffle of sneakers on the asphalt and the whistling of the wind. They felt hemmed in by the towering walls that lined the street.

The street led straight to a parking lot at the far end of the grounds, near the river. Larry stopped and slipped over to the side of the road, against a building. "Look out!" he whispered.

The gang froze as they spotted first the glowing red tip of a cigarette, then the guard leaning against one of the trucks in the parking lot. Luckily he was looking in the other direction. They shrank back into the shadows next to Larry and waited.

Diggy could feel Chessie's breath on his neck. He peered around the corner of the building at the guard. Move, he commanded silently. You're paid to guard this place, not goof off.

But the guard took his time, leaning against the side of the truck and watching the lights moving on the river. It seemed an eternity before he dropped his cigarette and crushed it underfoot. Then he stretched, adjusted his gunbelt, and strolled off. The gang waited two minutes before edging out of the shadows.

The parking lot was next to a large, long building with a high, curved roof. They approached it cautiously, glancing around, and then peered excitedly through one of the windows. It was very black inside, and they could see nothing.

"Someone shine the flashlight in there," Diggy ordered. Sphinx took a pen flashlight from his jacket pocket and shone the beam inside. Nothing but two or three large packing crates could be seen.

"I don't think that's it," Diggy said. "But there's got to be a clue here somewhere. We'll just have to check all the other buildings around here."

"Oh, no!" Chessie said. "It'd take days to search this whole place."

"Anyone got a better idea?" Diggy asked. No one volunteered. "Okay, then, let's get started. We're looking for a green glow, or for that thing Tilo and Sphinx saw. Something as big as that will be hard to hide. We'll stick together and look into all the windows." He pointed to a two-story brick building across the street. "And let's start with that one."

☐

With Larry mounting guard they crept over to the wall of the large brick building and peered through the barred windows. It was black inside, and all that could be seen were vague, bulky shapes, some that looked like large tanks, some like long, flat machines. They moved slowly along the wall from window to window, searching for a large black cylinder. There was nothing in the first building. The second, too, showed no sign of the mysterious UFO.

They had gone halfway down the wall of the third building when Chessie gasped and gripped Sphinx's arm. "I think I see something!" she whispered.

They peered through the window. There it was—the green glow—only now it seemed to be coming from inside a jagged crack that ran down the side of a cylindrical metal tank. The tank stood in the corner of a large room, on an elevated deck several feet above the floor. "Good going, Chessie," Diggy said.

"How do we get in?" Larry said. "Barred windows. The door must be locked." He went over and tried the bolt. "Yep, locked. And no fire escape. What now?"

"Let's look around the building and see if there's any other way in," Diggy said.

They spread out, circling the building. Diggy was halfway around when he heard Sphinx's hiss. "Psst! Over here!"

The gang gathered around a small shelter which stood off to one side of the storage building. It was an open structure, with just four supports in the ground and a wooden canopy overhead. Under the canopy was a metal railing. Sphinx shone his flashlight over the bars.

On the ground inside the railing was a circular metal door on hinges. "What's this?" Sphinx muttered.

"Do you think it leads into the building?" Diggy asked.

Larry shook his head. "I don't think so. This looks like the entrance to an underground storage tank. See those dials on the wall down there? That probably tells them how much there is in the tank."

"No help," Sphinx said. He backed away and stared at the building. "So what now?"

Diggy paused. "Well, if we can't get in ourselves, I guess we'll just have to get the guard to let us in. How does that sound?"

"Like you're off your rocker?" Sphinx offered.

"Nope. I have an idea. Everybody back behind that wall over there." Diggy pointed across the street. The rest of the gang looked at each other, then crossed the street, and ducked behind the wall. Diggy knelt down, searching the ground until he found what he wanted: a stone about the size of his fist. He stood up, hefting it in his hand. Then he backed off, and, gripping the stone firmly, leaned back, and threw it at a metal sign high on the wall of the building. Turning, he ran across the street and vaulted over the wall.

The crash of stone on metal was like an explosion, loud enough to be heard throughout the plant. The echo had barely died away when they heard the noise of running feet as the guard came to investigate. They huddled behind the wall, holding their breath. The guard went up to the door of the building. There was a silence. He must have decided that the noise had come from inside the building, because they heard the metallic click of a lock being turned, the squeal of the door opening—and silence.

Diggy waited, then stood up and whispered, "Let's go!" He vaulted the wall and ran toward the open door.

6

☐   Larry was the last to enter. He slipped through the door as quietly as he could, then joined the others as they crouched behind a nearby tank. The guard could be heard moving around on the second floor. Diggy peered around the side of the tank. The green glow could be seen faintly at the far end of the building.

"C'mon!" Diggy whispered and began to weave his way silently between the enormous storage tanks. The others followed. Sphinx had his pen flashlight out, and its narrow beam lit up their path.

Suddenly Diggy halted. He motioned to the others to come forward. "What's this?" he hissed.

They gathered around him, their eyes shining pale in the dim light. Diggy had bumped up against a steel railing that encircled a round metal plate set into the floor. Sphinx ran the flashlight beam over the plate. It was about four feet in diameter, with a heavy handle. "It's a door," he whispered.

Diggy glanced around. "Why would they have an exit like this here?"

"It must be a drainage tunnel," Larry whispered. "To flush waste out of the plant."

"Sssshhh," hissed Bobbie.

They paused, looking around. Diggy had begun to move on toward the far wall when all at once the darkness around them disappeared and a strong beam of light pinned them down.

"Who's that?" the guard shouted from the top of the stairway. "Stay where you are, do you hear me? Don't move!"

The teenagers stared, frozen. Then all five of them turned and bolted for the door.

"Stop!" cried the guard, coming after them. "Stop, do you hear?"

The five sprinted through the door. Diggy was the last one through. As he lunged outside he turned and pulled the door shut behind him and rammed the bolt home. From inside they could hear angry cries as the guard pounded on the heavy door.

"C'mon!" gasped Diggy. "C'mon! Run!"

As they ran through the dark streets of the plant grounds the cries of the guard faded rapidly behind them. But all at once a bell began to clang, louder and louder.

"Oh, no!" Larry groaned. "He's triggered the alarm!"

"Follow me," said Diggy. He raced back toward the main gate, retracing the way they came. The plant buildings rose up on either side, first dark, then bathed in light as a searchlight swept past them. The alarm bell was shrill in the distance.

"This way," Diggy gasped. He turned a corner, only to find two guards running down the street toward him. "Back!" he cried, dodging into an alleyway between two buildings. "C'mon!"

They scrambled down the alleyway, ducked around a corner, and flattened against the wall. Behind them the guards had stopped and were shining lights down the narrow passage.

"Did they go down here?" one of them asked.

There was a muttered reply. The light came closer and closer, sweeping the walls.

54

"Over here," Sphinx whispered. He slid back to the corner and peered around it. "Hurry!"

They fled around the far corner of the building as the guard shone his flashlight at the spot they had just left. They could hear him cursing.

"This way," hissed Sphinx. Edging down the passage, he reached the main street. He glanced up and down. "Okay, it's clear."

They scrambled out and were about to run when a dark figure stepped out of the shadows on the other side of the street. Before they could move, he had grabbed Chessie and was pinning her arms behind her back.

"Okay, kids," the guard said. "Stay where you are."

☐

"Mr. Sheaffer?" the guard said into the phone. "We have a problem here. Would you come over right away, sir? Yes. Thank you. Building Six."

He hung up and dialed another number. "Mr. Wood? Connors here. There's been a disturbance at the plant, sir. Building Six. Thank you."

The other guard was standing near the door of the warehouse, staring at the frightened teenagers, who were huddled together in an open area between two large crates.

Connors hung up and came over to them. "Initiation stunts for a gang, huh?" he growled. "Not too likely, if you ask me. The manager and foreman will be here in a few minutes."

Diggy did not bother to look up. The guards had herded them into the warehouse and questioned them sharply, and Diggy had told his story several times in the past fifteen minutes.

"I'm telling you, sir," Sphinx said, "we're trying to get into a gang at school. All five of us. We were told to sneak into a factory at night without getting caught."

"Well, you didn't do too well, kid," Connors said. "And you're not going to be trying out any more stunts—not around here, anyway."

Sphinx fell silent. The guard leaned back against the wall. There was a long pause.

Chessie leaned over to Diggy. "What are they going to do with us?" she whispered.

The boy shrugged. "What can they do?"

"Put us in jail!" she moaned.

"Don't worry, Chess, I have a feeling they won't call the police," Diggy replied. But he was not so sure. What *would* the manager and foreman do? And what would their parents say when they found out?

The guard sauntered over to the door to talk to his companion outside. Sphinx caught Diggy's eye and jerked his chin toward the right.

Diggy turned. On the wall to one side of the door was a panel with several large switches. When they had been pushed through the door, the warehouse had been dark. One of the guards must have pulled the switches. The lights had come on not only inside the warehouse but also in the streets outside, as Diggy could see through the window.

He nodded. "Wait for my move," he whispered.

There was the sound of voices outside. The guards came back into the room, followed by two other men. One was tall and long-nosed with dark hair. The other was of medium height, fat, and bald.

"What's this all about?" the fat man said.

"We found these kids hiding behind a storage tank in one of the buildings, Mr. Sheaffer," the guard replied. "They claim it was an initiation stunt for a school gang. I thought you'd want to question them."

"Right," said the manager. He came forward and glared at the gang. "Okay, who's gonna talk first?"

"Me," Diggy said.

"What's the real story, kid? Just out of curiosity, you understand. I'm gonna have all of you locked up, no matter what. Breaking and entering. Now, what're you doin' here?"

Diggy shook his head. "It was a gang initiation, sir. I kept telling the guard that, but he wouldn't believe me."

"Do you know what you've done?" Sheaffer asked. "You broke into this plant at night. Illegal entry. I don't care if you *are* just a bunch of kids, I'm gonna prosecute, you understand? This ain't no kid's game. Now, let's have the truth."

Diggy was silent. He sat down on a box and looked away.

The man leaned closer to him. "I'm the manager here and I'm telling you, I'm going to have you all locked up for this. Now, are you gonna tell me or not? What were you really doing? In two minutes I'm callin' the cops."

Diggy looked up at him. Then he turned, went over to the phone, and held the receiver out to Sheaffer.

"Okay," he said, "why don't you call the police? We'll tell them our story, just as we've told you. As a matter of fact, why don't you ask for Sergeant Gauss? He's a friend of ours. I'm sure he'd be glad to come down here and talk to you."

"You're crazy, kid," the manager growled. "You're right, that's what I'm gonna do: call the cops right now."

Diggy was still holding the phone out. "Well, why don't you?"

The manager glanced at the foreman, who was standing next to the guards, watching him.

"Shut up and put the phone down, kid," Sheaffer

snapped. He went over to the foreman for a brief, muttered conference in a corner of the room.

Diggy waited quietly with the phone in his hand. He glanced at the open door. The guards were leaning against the wall next to it. Diggy chewed his lip. No way to get out while they were blocking the door.

The gang had gathered in a loose group, watching him. He glanced meaningfully at the door again, trying to lead their eyes to it. None of the men really expected them to make a break for it—they were just a bunch of kids. But they had a good chance *if* Diggy could only get those guards away from the door.

He had a sudden inspiration. He turned, hanging up the phone with a click. The guards glanced at him and then began talking to each other. Diggy waited a moment. Then he snatched the phone off the hook and rapidly began to dial.

"Hello, Sergeant Gauss?" he cried. "Sergeant—"

"What's he doing? Stop him!" Sheaffer shouted. The guards turned and leaped forward, away from the door.

Diggy dropped the phone and ducked away. As he did, Sphinx sprang forward and pulled down all three light switches. The warehouse and the grounds outside were plunged into darkness.

"*Run!*" Sphinx cried, over the enraged shouts of the four men. Diggy felt a hand close around his arm. He fell, squirming away. Then he scrambled to his feet and ran for the door.

7

☐   Diggy made it to the door and, turning, dodged down a narrow alleyway just as the lights went on again all over the plant. The other members of the gang had already scattered, vanishing behind the buildings. Behind him he could hear the four men in the street, shouting to each other. He turned a corner and waited there, his heart pounding.

"Those rotten kids!" he could hear the manager say. "What do they think they're doing?"

"They can't get out," said one of the guards. "The front gate is closed."

"They could be anywhere," snapped the manager. "Connors, how many men are on duty tonight?"

"Four, sir."

"All right. I want you two to cover the front gate and make sure nobody slips through. Tell the others to search the plant. Get going. Those kids could be anywhere."

Their voices died away down the street. Diggy waited, his breath coming painfully. The manager was right; the other gang members must be scattered all over the plant. How would they ever get out?

And now there would be guards at the gate. He edged forward, going quickly and silently down the alleyway, and stuck his head around the edge of the building. He thought he remembered how to get back to the entrance, but if he could follow the guards, it would be that much easier. He could see the four men, their backs toward him, at the far end of the street.

He ran back down the narrow passage and began to follow them, keeping behind the buildings in the alleys which criss-crossed the plant grounds. He stayed parallel to the main street, about a hundred yards behind them. He knew that the warehouse had not been far from the main gate, and that the gang had been about halfway back from the far end of the plant when they had been caught. He only hoped that the others would be able to make their way to the meeting place.

He came forward again, crept down a passage, and peered into the street to check his bearings. They were gone! And the gate was nowhere in sight. He cursed silently.

Suddenly a hand dropped onto his shoulder.

"Wha . . . ?" gasped Diggy, whirling around.

Behind him, in the shadows, stood Chessie, her eyes wide and frightened. "I'm sorry!" she whispered.

"*Chess!* Where are the others?"

"I don't know. I got out the door and just ran."

"Okay," Diggy said. "Boy, am I glad to see you. We'll have to get back to the gate. I hope the others can, too."

"Sssshhhh," Chessie hissed. She pointed. "Look at that!" Diggy turned. There, down the street and to the left, a section of the plant had suddenly been flooded with light.

"Right," he muttered. "That must be the gate. Good, that makes it easy."

"Easy?" Chessie whispered. "*Easy?*"

"C'mon," Diggy said. He led the way down the passage and began to trot through the streets, keeping close to the buildings as he passed. Behind him Chessie followed, a quick, silent shadow.

As they headed for the lights they could hear the shouts of

the two guards, who were still searching the streets. Diggy turned left, quickening his pace, and the voices grew fainter as the guards moved away to another part of the plant.

Suddenly he stopped and crouched down. Chessie came up behind him.

"There," he whispered, pointing.

The alley widened in front of them to form a large open space. On the opposite side stood the gate, bathed in bright lights. Two men patrolled in front of it.

"Where's that little building?" Chessie murmured.

Diggy glanced around. The low wooden building they had agreed on as a meeting place was nowhere in sight.

"It was over to the left of the gate when we came in," Chessie whispered. "Do you think this might be a different gate?" She stood up and crept over to the other side of the passageway, disappearing into the shadows between two large buildings.

Diggy followed. Chessie was a small, dark figure, far down the alley. She paused, turning to make sure the guards could not see her. Then she sidled across the space between two buildings and stopped behind a wooden wall. Diggy joined her a moment later.

"This is it," she said, peering around the corner.

"Are you sure?" Diggy stared around him. His memories of entering the plant were confused. It seemed like a long time ago. "This is the one?"

"Uh-huh. Trust me."

"Okay. I hope the others can get back here."

"Yeah." Chessie paused, huddling against the wall. "Diggy?"

"Yeah?"

"I'm scared."

He leaned back against the wall, his arms crossed. That's nothing," he said. "*I'm* terrified."

◻

Sphinx, his hair bristling like a porcupine's, edged down one of the narrow alleyways. He had seen the lights go on in one section of the plant, and now he was trying to find his way there through the maze of buildings and streets. He sidled down the passage, feeling his way along the wall.

Suddenly a flashlight picked him out of the darkness.

"There's one of them!"

Sphinx stared, his eyes mirroring the light. Then he turned and was gone, racing down the street. There were shouts behind him.

"Stop! You there! *Stop!*"

He could hear shouts and the pounding of feet as the second guard joined the first. He dodged between the buildings, gasping, his heart thundering. At last he had to stop to get his breath. Leaning back against a wall, panting, he listened for sounds of pursuit. But there was silence behind him. The guards had gone off in the wrong direction.

Sphinx lifted a trembling hand and ran it through his hair. He tried to breathe deeply and easily. Gosh, that was close! He turned, searching through the darkness for the blaze of lights that signaled the front gate. There it was—farther away than ever. He sat down for a moment, until his heart had stopped racing, and tried to remember just where the meeting place was. Then he stood up with a sigh and began to trace his way back.

◻

Diggy and Chessie jumped as two figures loomed out of the darkness beside them. It was Larry and Bobbie.

"You okay?" Diggy whispered. They nodded, their faces white with strain. "Have you seen Sphinx?"

"No," Bobbie whispered. "We thought he'd be here already."

"What are we going to do?" Larry murmured. "There's no way out that gate."

They peered around the corner of the building. The two guards were still there and had been joined by the manager and foreman, who stood talking quietly. Diggy shook his head.

"Let me think," he said. "Let me think."

They huddled against the wooden wall and looked at each other. They felt trapped. How would they ever get out?

Suddenly, a tall, thin stick of a figure slipped across the passage toward them, talking in a low mumble as it approached.

"Sphinx!" said Diggy.

"Horrible," Sphinx said. "Horrible. I almost got caught, twice. The guards saw me. Then I got so confused I couldn't remember where this building was. Horrible."

The redhead leaned against the wall, breathing heavily. "No chance of escape by the front gate," he said. "Too many guards, too well lit."

"What're we going to do?" Bobbie whispered.

"They'll find us sooner or later," said Larry, his face pinched.

There was a silence. Diggy stood, thinking desperately. Larry was right: They would be found, and soon. Should they just give up and turn themselves in? But after all this . . .

"Wait a minute," he said slowly. "Remember? Inside the building with the storage vats. . . ."

He looked at Sphinx, who nodded.

"Of course," Sphinx whispered. "There *is* another exit—the drainage tunnel!"

"That's right," Chessie said. "And they'll never think of *that!*"

Diggy paused and looked around him. Then he nodded. "Okay," he snapped. "It's our only chance. C'mon!"

□

Ten minutes later they were standing around the entrance to the tunnel.

They had found their way there swiftly and surely, with no close escapes. All the guards were clustered at the front gate, on the lookout for the gang there. The door to the storage building had been left open.

"The guards ran out so fast, they forgot to lock it again," Bobbie said as they slipped through.

"Yeah, but we'd better hurry. Someone will remember, and they'll be back," Sphinx said.

"Now, what about that trapdoor?" Larry asked.

"Wait a minute," Diggy said. "Now that we've got the chance, we've got to get a look at that green glow before we leave. That's why we came, after all."

"We should get out of here right away," said Chessie.

"It'll just take a sec," Diggy replied. They threaded their way between the dark storage vats, heading for the far wall of the building. As they drew closer the ghostly green glow became brighter. Their faces shone weirdly in the light.

At last they found themselves by a large storage tank. Down its rounded sides curled several threads of a shining green substance. They looked up, in silence.

"So that's what it is—some kind of chemical," Sphinx said. "Nothing to do with aliens at all. Lots of chemicals glow in the dark."

"Do you think it's radioactive?" Chessie asked.

"No," Sphinx replied. "If it were, this tank would be covered with lead shields and there'd be warning signs all over it."

"We need a sample," Diggy said. "Larry? Do you have something to hold this stuff?"

"Sure." Larry knelt down, took out his penknife, and scraped some of the phosphorescent material into a small vial. He stood up and shoved the vial into his pocket.

"That's it," Diggy said. "Let's get out of here."

When they reached the tunnel again, Sphinx clambered over the railing like a huge spider. Reaching down, he grasped the handle, carefully lifting the heavy door on its hinges. It was completely black inside, and smelled damp and musty.

Sphinx took out his flashlight and flicked it on. The uncertain, wavering light showed a small ladder leading down into the darkness. The gang stared at it in silence.

"We don't even know where it goes," Bobbie said. "It could just lead to another part of the plant."

"Well, we're going to find out," Sphinx said. "Follow me." He swung himself down, grasping the ladder, and lowered himself into the tunnel. They could see the feeble light descending step by step.

"Okay," said Bobbie. She swung herself easily over the railing and disappeared down the ladder. One by one the others followed her.

They found Sphinx standing at the bottom, where the tunnel widened. His flashlight was focused on a small sign on the wall next to the ladder.

"Automatic waste disposal," he read. Then he shook his head. "Sure hope it doesn't dispose of any waste while we're still in here."

"Let's hurry," Diggy said. "Sphinx, you go first with the flashlight. Move as fast as you can."

They set off, half-crouching, their arms held out to balance themselves in the round tunnel. The ceiling was very low, and before they had gone far, their backs began to hurt. But there was no time to stop. They shuffled along in the darkness, whispering encouragement to each other. Sphinx and Larry were in the lead, followed by Chessie and Bobbie, with Diggy in the rear.

They stumbled along, following the faint beam of the flashlight. The walls were damp and foul-smelling, and the gang's backs and legs were soon aching. Still they moved on, their heads down, their hands bruised and scratched by the rough walls.

They had been in the tunnel for perhaps fifteen minutes, although it seemed much longer, when Diggy, at the end of the line, suddenly heard something behind him. He paused for a second, half-turning. It was a faint rumble, growing louder. He waited, listening—then he turned and scrambled toward the others.

"Sphinx!" he cried, his voice echoing oddly from the walls. "Sphinx! Hurry up! *They're flushing out the tunnel!*"

Sphinx paused and his flashlight flickered. Then it went on again, and they began moving twice as fast. Behind him the gang staggered through the blackness, their breath coming short and fast, their hands ripped and bleeding from the walls.

Chessie stumbled and almost lost her footing, sliding to one knee against the curved floor, flailing out with both arms. Behind her, Bobbie lifted her up and pushed her forward. As she hurried after Chessie, Bobbie almost fell herself.

"Hurry!" she urged. The two of them fled through the darkness.

"Sphinx! *Hurry!*" shouted Diggy, from behind.

The rumbling was louder now, echoing behind them. Diggy could hear the rushing of waste water as it poured from pipes all over the plant into the tunnel.

"*Sphinx!*" he shouted.

The roar of the water was deafening in the cramped space. Sphinx, in the lead, suddenly slipped and fell. Larry ran straight into him from behind. The flashlight flew out of Sphinx's hand, hit the wall with a dull thud, and went out. They were trapped in darkness!

"Oh, no!" Sphinx groaned, half-sobbing. He scrambled to his feet and groped about frantically for the flashlight. His fingers closed around it, and he flicked the switch, but there was no light. It was dead.

"Sphinx! Keep moving!" Larry cried, and gave him a push.

Sphinx reached out blindly in the darkness and went on. Behind him the others staggered along, gasping, the sound of the waste water loud behind them. The tunnel was beginning to fill with a terrible stench, and they started to cough, their eyes watering, as they ran.

"This is it," Diggy thought confusedly. "This is it . . . there's no way out. . . !"

Suddenly the line halted. Sphinx had stopped and was shouting something, his words lost in the roar of the water and their own hoarse coughing.

". . . *out* . . ." Diggy heard him cry. "Grate. . . !"

"Sphinx!" he screamed. "What is it?"

Sphinx's words were unintelligible. "Back!" he cried. "Back . . .!" The rest of what he said was lost.

Bobbie turned around. "Move *back!*" she shouted at Diggy. "There's a grate blocking the exit! Move *back!*"

Diggy stumbled backward. At the front of the line Sphinx took a few steps back and then made a flying leap. His shoulder hit the grating, which shook, but held in place.

"Let me try," gasped Larry. He leaned forward and shook the grating, feeling for weak spots. There was a rusty area on one side. He leaned his shoulder against it and pushed. Sphinx moved behind him and added his weight.

The sound of the water was fearsomely close now, pouring through the tunnel. "No good!" Larry gasped, shaking the bars in frustration. "No good! Move back!"

Sphinx fell back, and Larry braced himself. He ran forward, hitting the grate, which groaned but held in place.

"Again!" cried Sphinx, behind him.

Larry scrambled away from the opening and then threw himself against it. The iron bars shook but held.

There was a dull pain in Larry's shoulder. For the third time he moved back and braced himself, then desperately threw all his weight forward. He hit the iron grating—

And suddenly found himself catapulted out of the tunnel and rolling down a hill of wet mud!

Behind him Sphinx came flying out of the opening. Larry began to scramble up the riverbank.

"Quick!" he gasped. "Quick! Help the others!"

The two of them pulled themselves up the slope on their hands and knees. At the same time the two girls fell out of the tunnel and began to tumble down toward the river.

Sphinx tackled Chessie, while Larry scooped up Bobbie, pulling her over to one side. Above them Diggy fell out of the hole.

"*Ow!*" he cried, reaching out to clutch at a clump of weeds as he rolled down the slippery bank. Sphinx ran forward, grabbing him and pushing him to one side.

They had barely gotten out of the way before the tunnel echoed with an ominous, rumbling sound. Suddenly a flood of dirty brown water shot out and plunged down to the river!

8

☐   Sphinx," said Diggy, "wake up!"

He nudged his friend, whose tousled red hair was buried in his arms on the desk.

"Leave me alone," said a muffled voice. "Let me sleep."

"Sphinx, class is about to start. Mr. Dawson'll appreciate it if you're awake."

"Mr. Dawson should appreciate what I did for him," Sphinx said in a hollow voice. He lifted his head and glared around him. "He should be grateful."

"That was Saturday, Sphinx. Two nights ago. Why are you still such a mess?"

"Homework," Sphinx explained. "I slept all day yesterday after we got back. So I had to stay up all last night doing my math homework. It's not fair. I'll never return to normal time."

"Well, you always said you wanted to be nocturnal, like a bat."

"Yeah, but at least bats *sleep* during the day. I feel like going off somewhere and hanging upside down from the ceiling for a few hours."

Mr. Dawson came into the classroom and the whispering stopped. All the students stared. Ever since the rumors had started, their teacher had become an object of curiosity. No one said anything in front of him, but the whole school still buzzed with stories.

He went to the front of the room, put his papers down on the desk, and with a wan smile, began his lecture. Diggy scribbled notes while Sphinx's head slowly lowered itself toward the desk. By the time class was over, he was sound asleep.

"Sphinx," said Diggy, giving him a push, "you're hopeless. C'mon, time for math."

"Math?" Sphinx's head came up with a start. "Math? Good . . . I can hand in my homework and then sleep with a clear conscience."

They gathered up their notebooks and began to leave. On their way out Mr. Dawson called them over.

"Sorry to disturb you, boys," he said, looking up from a pile of papers, "but I did notice, Sphinx, that you were having a little trouble concentrating today. That is to say, you were asleep. Am I boring you, or is something else the matter?"

"No, no," Sphinx mumbled, looking down at his feet. "It's nothing, Mr. Dawson. Just some math homework I had to stay up late to finish. See?" He produced three pages of illegibly scrawled equations.

"Yes, well, try to get some more sleep, okay, Sphinx? The details of mitosis are difficult enough to learn even with your eyes open." He smiled and waved them off.

"Clever," Sphinx growled, once they were out in the hallway. "Clever. Even with your eyes open. If he only knew what we were doing for him!"

"Oh, come on, Sphinx. Anyone else would have given you heck for sleeping through the whole class the way you did today."

Sphinx sighed. "True enough," he said, tucking his homework back into his notebook. "True enough. Just wait and see what Mr. Henderson says."

☐

At lunchtime the whole gang gathered in the cafeteria. Tilo was there as well, furious at having missed the adventure in the chemical plant.

"I can't believe it," he said mournfully. "Just because I had to stay with my brother! You have all the fun, and I baby-sit."

Chessie stared at him.

"All the what?" she said. "You call being chased through a maze by gunmen and almost being drowned in an underground tunnel *fun?* I wish you had been there instead of me!"

"Me, too," said Larry, and the others nodded.

"We should have sent Tilo, and the rest of us could have stayed home and watched TV with his little brother," Bobbie suggested with a grin.

"Enough of that," Diggy said. "What do we do next?"

Everyone groaned.

"I can't even think about it," Chessie complained. "I've never been so cold and wet and scared in my whole life. Thank goodness my mother didn't catch me when I came in. She wouldn't have believed it."

"Mine almost did catch me," Bobbie said, "but I locked myself in the bathroom and took a shower for about three hours. She got bored and went away."

Larry lifted his hands, which, like the others', were still scratched and raw from the flight through the tunnel.

"These used to be the delicate hands of an artist," he said. "Look at them now."

"And mine!"

"And mine!"

"And my shoulder is still killing me," said Larry.

"Enough complaints," Diggy said. "Let's go over what we've found out. We know now that Twitchell is somehow involved with whatever's going on in Tinicum Swamp. And we know that the green glow is caused by that chemical. Larry, how can we find out what it is?"

"I thought Sphinx might bring it over to his professor friend," Larry said. He took the vial out. Diggy glanced over at Sphinx.

"Will someone please wake him up?" he said. "I'm tired of doing it. He's getting mean."

"Leave me alone!" Sphinx complained. "You have no right to disturb me. Haven't I suffered enough?" He lifted his head and blinked sleepily around him. "I had a dream," he said. "A wonderful dream. I was a bat . . . a vampire bat. I slept during the day, and at night I drank blood." He looked down at his cherry soda. "Aha."

"Sphinx," said Diggy, "do you have any suggestions, or do you just want to sleep all day?"

"I have a suggestion," said the boy. "I vote that we don't go to the plant next Saturday night. Or ever again, for that matter."

"That's not the point, Sphinx. Can you ask Professor Larsen to have the sample of that green stuff checked out in the chem lab at the university?"

Sphinx blinked. "Sure. I'll take it over there today."

"Okay. Now, we know that Twitchell's involved, that the green glow comes from some kind of chemical . . ."

"And that the light area in the photos must be the engine of the tanker truck," Larry interrupted. "I realized that last

73

night. That cylindrical object was a tanker, and infrared photos pick up heat sources, like a hot engine."

"Then the sound on the tape was probably the truck shifting gears, just before it left," Bobbie put in.

Diggy nodded. "Right. So what's going on in Tinicum Marsh?"

There was a pause. The gang members looked at each other.

"I think there's only one thing it could be," Chessie said firmly. "Pluto Research Company is dumping that green stuff into the stream illegally. That'd explain everything— the fact that they do it at night, that they're unwilling to call the police, all the recent 'UFO' sightings in this area—"

"*And* why Twitchell is so nervous," Bobbie put in. "No wonder he's so angry at Mr. Dawson—what if this all came out, about his connection with Pluto Research and everything? He'd be sunk!"

"Right," said Diggy. "I agree, that's what it must be. But all we have are a few blurry photos, a tape of grinding gears, and a sample of green stuff. What are we going to do?"

"I think it's time to tell the police what's going on," Chessie said.

"Yeah, but we don't have any proof, Chess. And we're just a bunch of kids. Why should they believe us?"

"They'd believe someone older," Bobbie said. "Maybe we should just go ahead and tell our parents?"

There was a silence. Chessie shuddered.

"I can't say I'm looking forward to that," she said. "My parents would have a fit."

"Mine, too," Larry said, and the others nodded.

"How about going to see the judge?" Tilo suggested.

"He'd listen to our story."

"That's a good idea!" Bobbie said. "The police would believe *him*."

"Oh, he's going to blow his top," Larry warned. "He told us to stay out of trouble, remember?"

Diggy sighed. "Okay. I'll go there after school today. Although I can't say I'm going to enjoy having to explain the whole thing to him." He glanced up as the bell rang. "Time for fourth period. Will somebody please wake Sphinx up?"

□

The judge stared at the boy seated in the big leather armchair opposite him.

"You mean to tell me, Diggy," he said, "that you and your friends actually went to this chemical plant, broke in during the night, were caught, and then managed to escape . . . through a *tunnel?*"

Diggy looked uncomfortable.

"I'm afraid so," he said. "Ahead of a wall of water. It was really exciting. Something I hope will never happen to me again—ever."

The judge leaned back and sighed.

"The whole story is fantastic, Diggy. The police will never believe it. I'm not sure that *I* believe it. Haven't I warned you about taking the law into your own hands? That computer business last month was bad enough. This time you might have been killed. These harebrained escapades! When are you going to learn?"

He got up and paced about the room. Diggy watched him from the shelter of the chair. The judge was really angry.

"You, all of you, broke the law," he said, stopping in front of Diggy's chair. "The penalty for breaking and entering is severe. I won't have any more of this, Diggy! I won't be an accomplice to a crime. This was no mere joke."

"But, sir, that's just the point—we wouldn't have been arrested. The manager had no intention of calling the police. We could have stayed and bluffed it out, I guess, but all we thought of at the time was getting away. He doesn't want the police called in, because there's something illegal going on in there. That's why you've got to get Sergeant Gauss and his people to believe us."

The judge frowned and continued his restless pacing. There was a long silence. Diggy, crouched in his chair, watched the older man's face.

Finally the judge came back and sat down wearily in his armchair. "And you think Twitchell is involved with the Pluto company?"

"That's right, sir."

The judge sighed. "Are you sure, Diggy?"

"Chessie heard him talking to someone on the telephone about how much he was doing for Pluto."

The judge shook his head. "So he's mixed up in this, too. And he's the one who's been hounding Mr. Dawson. Well, it makes sense, Diggy. But for real proof, these people have to be caught dumping that material into the river. And we'll have to be very, very sure, Diggy. You can't move against a prominent politician without proof."

He leaned back and stared off into space. The clock on the mantelpiece ticked loudly in the waiting silence.

"Have you told anyone else about this?"

The boy shook his head. "We figured you'd be able to advise us."

The judge smiled. "A little bit of flattery, eh? Well, I'm

not going to help you because of that, boy. All those years on the bench have only made me suspicious of compliments. There's only one reason in all of this that might possibly make me want to help you out of this mess you're in."

Diggy leaned forward. "What's that, sir?"

"Your teacher, Mr. Dawson. If you and your friends are right about all this, then he's been treated very shabbily by the school administration, the school board, and the community at large. He did see something in the swamp after all. It's not true what people are saying about him, and what he's telling himself—that he's been having hallucinations because of what happened to him in Vietnam. That's the reason—and, I might add, the only reason—that I am willing to become involved in this whole affair. Do you understand me, Diggy?"

"Yes, sir."

The judge glared at him. "Well, I certainly hope so. You and your friends are ruining my credibility. I don't know whether Sergeant Gauss will believe this story even from me." He picked up the telephone and dialed.

□

The heavy-set police officer hunched forward in his chair and shook his head in disbelief.

"He *what?*" he said into the phone. "He *what?*"

He paused, listening. Then, with a choking sound, he stabbed a pencil into his desk blotter and broke it in two. He flung it aside and reached for another.

"They *what?*" he said in disgust. "For God's sake, judge, why didn't you . . . oh . . . oh, I see. . . ." The second pencil broke with a loud snap. "Yes, yes. *What?* I don't believe it. This is the limit, judge. I . . . what? Okay. Okay, yes, I'll get back to you. Yes, fine, I understand." He started to hang up and then grasped the receiver again. "Judge? Is he still there? Okay, I want you to do two things for me. One, ask the kid to give me the photos and a map of where they were taken. And, two, please bind and gag him and all his friends. *All* of them. Yes. Thank you very much." He banged down the telephone.

□

"Was he upset?" asked Diggy.

The judge turned from the phone, a faint smile on his lips.

"I don't know if you'd call it upset, exactly," he said. "I'd call it 'murderous.' He's in charge now, Diggy. You and I have nothing to do but wait. Oh, yes, he'd like to see the photos and a map of the swamp after school tomorrow."

"He's going to check it out?" Diggy asked eagerly.

"Yes, but it'll take a while. They'll have to catch these people in the act. You should have some idea how long that might take."

Diggy groaned, thinking of the fruitless night he and Chessie had spent in the swamp. Then he paused as a sudden thought startled him. He stared at the judge.

What if the manager of the plant realized that someone was onto them? What if the Pluto Research Company simply stopped dumping waste in Tinicum Marsh? The whole case would be finished!

9

☐ "This is the worst map I've ever seen," said Sergeant Gauss. He lifted the piece of paper and inspected it. "I couldn't find my own house with a map like this. And these photos are useless. Do you have anything else?"

"I can't really draw," said Diggy apologetically. "So I brought along this city map, too." He took it out of his pocket and spread it out on the table. "This should show you where it is. See, here's the bus stop we used, and here's the stream, and here's where it widens out and then curves around a bend. And this is the spot where they dump the waste."

The police officer grunted. He marked the place with a red pencil and examined the map.

"Okay, kiddo," he said. "That'll do it. The other guys around here can't believe that I'm listening to a bunch of kids. . . . But one thing about all this puzzles me. I checked with the Essington police, and they have no report from this Pluto Research Company about a break-in. Very odd. Still, I don't like the fact that you think this politician is involved. Can't you just go play stickball or something and leave this kind of stuff to us?"

"So you'll be watching the swamp tonight, sergeant?"

"Yeah, just in case. We'll stake out the place and see if there's any activity. You might have frightened them off by breaking into the plant, you know. It could be a while before they're brave enough—or stupid enough—to try again."

"I'm sorry," Diggy said. "We thought we'd be able to get

some proof that way. Which reminds me: Here's a sample of that chemical we found in the plant. Sphinx had it analyzed by a friend of his. He said it's called phenotryl, and it's a by-product of a process to produce high-strength plastic." Diggy placed the vial on the desk. "Don't spill it on your skin or breathe it—it's very toxic."

"Okay. Not that that proves anything. It's not surprising that a chemical plant would have luminous waste in it. I thought of alerting the health and safety inspectors, but I figured Pluto Research is sure to have a good story about how they're getting rid of it. If they *are* dumping it, then they're saving themselves a lot of money. It costs a lot to have it disposed of legally. They'd have to put it in burst-proof steel drums and pay to have it buried at an approved site. They must be making a bundle right now."

Diggy nodded and stood up to leave. "So you'll let me and the judge know just as soon as you catch them?" he asked eagerly. "Mr. Dawson's about to lose his job over this. The principal and Mr. Twitchell are trying to force him to resign."

The police officer stared at him. "I can't believe this," he said. "The judge calls me yesterday with this lame-brained story, I take a day to get organized, and now a thirteen-year-old kid is telling me to hurry up?"

Diggy grinned. "Thanks, sergeant," he said and hurried off.

□

The next day was Wednesday, the date of the school board meeting. During biology class Mr. Dawson was distracted and confused. He would pause in the middle of a sentence and look blankly out at the class before he remembered where he was. Diggy and Sphinx glanced at each other.

"He's scared," Sphinx whispered. "The board is out for blood, they say."

Diggy shook his head and looked down at his notebook, which today was filled with scribbles, crossed-out sentences, and aimless doodles. He was as distracted as his teacher.

Sphinx scrawled *When will you hear?* on a scrap of paper and passed it over. Diggy glanced at it, shrugged, and scribbled *I hope at lunchtime* on a note that he slipped back.

"Not a moment too soon," Sphinx muttered. "The meeting is this afternoon."

"Oliver," Mr. Dawson's voice broke in, "I hate to interrupt you, but I was wondering whether you would mind sharing with the class the answer to question nine?"

Sphinx goggled at him. "Not at all. The answer to question nine is . . ."—he squinted at his notebook—"telophase."

"That's right." Mr. Dawson sounded slightly surprised. "Thank you, Oliver."

Diggy sighed. Sphinx threw him a triumphant glance. "Only six more classes to go," he whispered, shutting his notebook with a thump.

□

When the bell for the lunch hour sounded, Diggy hurried out of class and ran for the telephone. He fumbled for a dime, then dialed the number of the police station.

"Hello? Hello, is Sergeant Gauss there, please? This is Diggy Caldwell speaking."

He waited, drumming nervously on the top of his notebook. Finally a deep voice answered.

"Gauss here."

"Sergeant? It's me, Diggy. What happened?"

There was a pause. "Nothing, Diggy. Nothing, except that I'm very tired today. You're sure that was the right spot?"

Diggy sagged against the side of the phone booth. "Yes, yes, I'm sure. Nothing? They didn't come?"

"Not a sign of them. Lots of wildlife, though. And I'm being teased like crazy around here. But don't worry, kid, we'll be there again tonight. It's been four days since you broke into the plant. They may have decided it was just a prank after all."

"Okay. Thanks, sergeant. And please . . . please let me hear the minute you find out. Thanks." Diggy hung up and stood for a moment, staring at the phone. They had no proof, nothing. And the school board was meeting today.

"We can't delay them?" demanded Chessie, at lunch.

"Have you ever tried delaying a school board meeting?" asked Sphinx. "You might as well throw yourself in front of a herd of stampeding elephants."

"'They also serve who only stand and wait,'" quoted Larry. "John Milton."

"We can't do a thing," said Diggy. "Larry's right. We've just got to give the police another day and see what they come up with."

"But you *know* they're going to fire Mr. Dawson this afternoon!" Bobbie exclaimed.

"I know," Diggy replied. "It's not fair. But there's nothing else we can do now . . . except, of course, pray that the Pluto Research Company is planning a trip out to the swamp tonight."

"But, you know, Diggy," Larry put in, "I don't think

we're being fair. We can't help the police—but there's something else we could do."

"What's that?"

"We could tell Mr. Dawson what we've seen and what happened in the plant. It won't make any difference to the school board—they won't listen to anyone but the police, anyway—but it'd sure make a difference to Mr. Dawson. He'd know he wasn't crazy, just seeing things in the swamp."

"You're right," Diggy said. The others were nodding. "The judge told me not to tell anyone else about this, but since the meeting is today . . ."

"Someone should go tell him," Bobbie cut in.

"Okay," Diggy said. "Who's free next period?"

They all shook their heads, except for Sphinx, who looked up from his hoagie, munching.

"There is one drawback," he said, indistinctly. "It'll get his hopes up. Then, if the police don't catch anyone, he'll be doubly disappointed."

"Yeah, but at least he'll know he wasn't hallucinating. That's worth it, isn't it?" Chessie asked.

"I dunno," mumbled Sphinx, getting to his feet. "Seems to me he might just figure we're as crazy as he is."

□

". . . and so you went out into the swamp, just to check my story?" Mr. Dawson shook his head. "I don't believe it," he murmured. "So what I saw was actually a tanker dumping something into the stream? Something that glowed in the dark?"

"That's right," Sphinx said. "Maybe we should have told you before this, but we decided to wait and try to get some real proof."

Mr. Dawson nodded. "You've seen what happens if you tell people stories like this without any evidence," he said, sighing.

"You know, Mr. Dawson, if you thought it would help, Tilo and I would be glad to go into the school board meeting with you and tell them what we saw in the swamp."

The man shook his head. "I appreciate the offer," he said, "but the board members will be sure that I forced you to go in and tell a crazy story—that I bribed you with grades or something like that. Or just that you're willing to lie to keep me here. And I'd rather not tip off that man Twitchell that anyone else has seen the dumping in the swamp."

"Well," said the boy, "maybe the police will come up with something tonight."

Mr. Dawson nodded. "And meanwhile," he said, "I owe you a great deal for coming and telling me this. It makes me almost willing to face the dragons today."

□

"Did you hear what happened?" Chessie demanded into the phone. She was eating dessert with one hand and holding the receiver with the other.

"Yeah, the whole school knows about it," Diggy said, on the other end. "'Scuse me, Chess . . . No, Mom, I don't want any more. Thanks. I'm just going to close the door here. Okay, Chess," he said, "I can talk now."

"They forced him to resign!" she went on. "Right on the spot. It's so unfair, Diggy. Here he's losing his job for something that isn't his fault at all."

"And we're the only ones who know about it," Diggy said. "And no one will believe us, even if we told them. I know, Chessie, I feel bad, too. But maybe Sergeant Gauss will see something tonight."

"Well, at least Sphinx got to him before the meeting," Chessie said. "Bobbie saw Mr. Dawson afterwards and said he took it real calmly. He said the thing that had been worrying him most was the fear that he was having another nervous breakdown, like after Vietnam."

"Well, I feel sorry for him," Diggy said. "But there's one other person I feel worse for, right now."

"Who's that?"

"Me," said Diggy. "If those people from Pluto Research don't show up tonight, Sergeant Gauss is going to skin and roast me alive. This could be my last night on earth, Chess."

"You think you've got a problem. The sergeant is supposed to be having dinner with my family this weekend. First he'll tell my parents all about it, and then they'll kill me."

"Great. Well, this has been a really uplifting conversation. I have to go now. My parents are frothing at the door. So long, Chess."

"See you tomorrow!"

□

"Sphinx," Diggy said, "wake up!"

Sphinx raised his head and sat up with a jerk, blinking. "What? What is it?"

"Twice in the same week, Sphinx. You're a basket case. What was it this time?"

Sphinx sighed. "Book report," he said, reaching into his folder. "Melville." He took out five pages of illegible script. "See? I hate Melville. I put it off past the late-late show. Then I had to stay up all night to finish it."

"I don't know how to break this to you, Sphinx, but our book reports aren't due today. They're due *next* Thursday. You got the week wrong."

The redhead stared at him. "You're kidding," he said. "I'm going to kill myself."

"Ssssshhhh," said Diggy. "Not now. Here comes Mr. Dawson."

The whole class turned, but the man who came in the door was not their teacher. He went to the front of the class and smiled.

"Mr. Dawson won't be in today," he said. "I'm Mr. Pell, your substitute teacher."

Diggy and Sphinx stared at each other. Mr. Dawson not in! Even if he was fired, he wouldn't have left that quickly—would he?

Sphinx shook his head and took out his biology notebook. "Nothing from Sergeant Gauss?" he whispered.

"He told me to call sometime this morning. I thought I'd try after class."

The other boy nodded. "Keep me informed," he said. "Things are getting awfully exciting around here."

□

Right after class Diggy raced for the hall telephone. He closed the door and hastily dialed the sergeant's number.

"Hello? This is Diggy Caldwell. Is Sergeant Gauss—oh . . . oh, I see. He just went out? Do you know where? . . . Oh, I see . . . okay. Okay, yes, thank you. No, just tell him I called. . . . Thanks. Thanks. Good-bye."

He hung up and leaned against the wall. Sergeant Gauss wasn't in, and no one knew where he had gone.

He left the phone booth and was shuffling along to his next class when he heard a familiar voice call his name.

"Diggy! Diggy, wait a minute!"

He turned around. It was Mr. Dawson . . . and right next to him was Sergeant Gauss!

The two men came down the hallway toward him. "No time to talk," said Mr. Dawson, grasping his hand. "Thank you. We're on our way to see Mr. Stevens."

Diggy looked up at the police officer.

"You mean you . . ."

Gauss nodded. "We got'em. Bunch of idiots. We had different parts of the swamp staked out, but they came right back to the same place. Nice job, kid. The map wasn't bad." He and the teacher strode off down the hall. "Not that I appreciate your harebrained stunts, kiddo!" Gauss shot back over his shoulder. "I have you to thank for two nights' missed sleep."

Then they were gone.

Mr. Stevens looked up from his desk as the two men came into his office. He gave the younger man a startled glance. "Dawson, what is this . . .?"

"I'm Sergeant Gauss, Tenth Precinct," interrupted the police officer. "Mr. Stevens, I have a story I think you should hear."

10

☐ "So the district attorney is going to move against Pluto Research for illegal dumping," Chessie said.

"That's right," said Diggy. "Sergeant Gauss said they'd probably get off with a heavy fine. But at least Mr. Dawson won't lose his job now."

"It was decent of Mr. Stevens to tell the whole story in front of the school assembly," Tilo said. The gang nodded.

"And did you hear the latest?" asked Bobbie with a laugh. "Twitchell has resigned from the school board!"

"No!" Chessie said. "When did you hear that?"

"Today, after school," said Bobbie, taking a slice of apple walnut cake. "Mr. Dawson told me. It seems that when the *real* story of what happened in Tinicum Marsh started getting around, and everyone knew the D.A. was getting into the act, Twitchell got nervous. Mr. Stevens got a call from him yesterday. Twitchell said he was too busy to continue to carry out his duties as a member of the school board. Can you believe it? He's coming up for reelection, you know. He has to be careful."

Larry shook his head. "I'm going to tell my parents not to vote for him," he said. "I wish we could prove he knew about the dumping."

"There's no proof, but there are a lot of rumors," Bobbie said. "People know he defended Pluto Research at that trial. He's going to have a lot of explaining to do."

"And the important thing is that Mr. Dawson's job is safe," Sphinx said.

The gang was gathered at Chessie's house for Sunday brunch. Her parents had helped her prepare the meal and then had left them alone. The Galaxy Gang was celebrating its triumph.

"Well, all I can say is that I hope our next case doesn't involve any swamps," Diggy remarked.

"Or drainage tunnels!" Chessie said.

"Or unidentified flying objects," said Tilo with a grin.

"*I* don't," said Sphinx, his mouth full of toast. There was a shocked silence.

"You don't?" Bobbie cried.

"Nope," Sphinx said. He took a gulp of soda. "Next time, I hope there really are little blue men with funny suits from the Crab Nebula. I hope there are twice as many tunnels to get through. I hope we have to sit in swamps that are wetter and colder than Tinicum was."

"But, Sphinx," said Chessie, with a burst of laughter, "why?"

"Because next time," said Sphinx, helping himself to a huge piece of cake, "I'm sending Tilo along instead of me! He's the brave one anyway," he added.

There was an explosion of cheers and shouts, and the gang lifted their glasses of soda.

"I propose a toast," Sphinx cried. "Here's to no more swamps!"

"*No more swamps!*" they chorused.

"And no more UFOs!" said Larry.

"*No more UFOs!*"

"And no more tunnels!" added Bobbie.

"*No more tunnels!*"

"And no more excitement . . . at least, for a while!" cried Diggy.

"*Cheers!*"

ABOUT THE AUTHORS

MILTON DANK grew up in Philadelphia, attended the University of Pennsylvania, from which he holds a doctorate in physics, and has worked as a research physicist in the aerospace industry.

Mr. Dank has written several novels for young adult readers, including *The Dangerous Game*, *Game's End*, *Khaki Wings*, and *Red Flight Two*. *The Computer Caper* and its companion novel, *A UFO Has Landed*, written in collaboration with his daughter Gloria, are the first two books in the Galaxy Gang Mystery series.

GLORIA DANK was graduated from Princeton University with a bachelor's degree in psychology and has worked as a computer analyst.

Milton Dank and Gloria Dank live in suburban Philadelphia.

Books Weekly Reader Books Weekly Reader